BATMAN LI'L GOTHAM

CALENDAR DAZE

Tuesday

BATMAN LI'L GOTHAM
CALENDAR DAZE

DUSTIN NGUYEN
DEREK FRIDOLFS
writers

DUSTIN NGUYEN
artist & colorist

SAIDA TEMOFONTE
letterer

DUSTIN NGUYEN
collection & original series cover artist

BATMAN created by
BOB KANE with BILL FINGER

SARAH GAYDOS
KRISTY QUINN
Editors - Original Series
ROBIN WILDMAN
Editor - Collected Edition
STEVE COOK
Design Director - Books
CURTIS KING JR.
Publication Design
CHRISTY SAWYER
Publication Production

MARIE JAVINS
Editor-in-Chief, DC Comics

DANIEL CHERRY III
Senior VP - General Manager
JIM LEE
Publisher & Chief Creative Officer
JOEN CHOE
VP - Global Brand & Creative Services
DON FALLETTI
VP - Manufacturing Operations & Workflow Management
LAWRENCE GANEM
VP - Talent Services
ALISON GILL
Senior VP - Manufacturing & Operations
NICK J. NAPOLITANO
VP - Manufacturing Administration & Design
NANCY SPEARS
VP - Revenue

BATMAN: LI'L GOTHAM: CALENDAR DAZE

DC Comics, 2900 West Alameda Ave., Burbank, CA 91505

Printed by Worzalla,
Stevens Point, WI, USA. 8/13/21.
First Printing.
ISBN: 978-1-77951-341-0

Library of Congress Cataloging-in-Publication Data is available.

GOTHAM

CONTENTS

HALLOWEEN

THAT'S BEEN ON ALL NIGHT, HASN'T IT?
THIS IS THE ONE NIGHT OF THE YEAR THAT IT STAYS ON UNTIL IT BURNS OUT.
IT'S A GOOD THING YOU'RE RICH ENOUGH TO AFFORD THE ELECTRIC BILL.
BUT I... DON'T...
SHUSH! DOWN THERE!
IT'S CRIME TIME.

FWUMP
AAGGGHHH! DON'T HURT US!
ROBIN-- STOP!!
THEY'RE JUST KIDS.
THEY'RE JUST KIDS... KIDS?! WHAT LOWLIFE HAS KIDS DOING THEIR DIRTY WORK?
AND BEFORE YOU ANSWER...I'M NOT A KID!

LOOK AROUND YOU. IT'S HALLOWEEN.
BUS
THERE'S NO TELLING WHO'S REAL AND WHO'S NOT...
FOR ALL I KNOW, MOST OF THESE COSTUMED JOKERS *ARE* THE REAL DEAL.
QUIT THAT!
TUGG

HAVEN'T YOU EVER CELEBRATED HALLOWEEN?
Hmmm...
"THE ONLY TIME I EVER CELEBRATED ANYTHING WITH FAMILY WAS WHEN MOM AND GRANDPA WOULD TEST OUT THE LAZARUS PIT BY DUMPING DEAD BODIES IN IT.
"FIGHTING OFF CRAZY REANIMATED ZOMBIES...THOSE WERE GOOD TIMES!
WHAT'S THE PURPOSE OF HALLOWEEN ANYWAYS?
IT'S A HOLIDAY TRACING BACK MANY YEARS. A WAY TO CELEBRATE PAGAN HARVESTS, THE END OF THE SEASON, OR EVEN FESTIVALS FOR THE DEAD.
A TIME WHEN THE PHYSICAL AND SUPERNATURAL WORLD WOULD BE AT THEIR CLOSEST POINT, TO CREATE MAGIC.
OKAY, FINE... IT'S ABOUT DRESSING UP AND GETTING CANDY.
NOW YOU'RE TALKIN'!
CALC+
THE STREETS OF GOTHAM

WAIT, WHAT ARE YOU--

SWEET
KRASH

NO.

HEH HEH HEH.

WHOA!
THOP

NO!
BET NIGHTWING DOES THAT ALL THE TIME.

YOU'RE GOING ABOUT THIS ALL WRONG.
YOU HAVE TO GO DOOR-TO-DOOR AND SAY THE WORDS "TRICK OR TREAT" TO GET YOUR CANDY.
THAT SOUNDS STUPID.

JUST TRY IT.

SO, GALLIANO'S ITALIANO? SEE YOU THERE...AND BRING EVERYONE.

SO... HOW DID IT GO?
ONE.
LOUSY.
PIECE.

HARDLY SEEMS WORTH IT. STILL...

HOLD IT!
WE'VE BEEN OUT ALL NIGHT. WE SHOULD GRAB DINNER FIRST, BEFORE YOU HAVE YOUR DESSERT.
YOU TAKE THE FUN OUT OF EVERYTHING.

WHEN THE GAS HITS YOUR EYE LIKE A BIGGA PIZZA PIE, THAT'S ARKHAMY...
MAMA MIA! YOUR'A ONE HOT'A SPICY MEATBALL!
AWWW, PUDDIN'.
SO...NO SALAD FOR YOU, HUH?
NOM NOM... MOPE!
I WISH HALLOWEEN WAS EVERY DAY OF THE YEAR.
THAT WAY, WE'D BE ABLE TO EAT OUT LIKE NORMAL FOLK AND FIT IN.
HEAR, HEAR!
DINGG

STRETCH
SLURRPP
BLOOOP
GULP
MOLTO BUONO!
THE REAL BATMAN HAS LONGER EARS. AND WHEN DID ROBIN START WEARING A HOOD?
OHHH, I GET IT. ROBIN HOOD... CLEVER.
WILL YOU BE DINING IN?
TWO CALZONES FOR TAKE-OUT.

OH, THAT'S TOO MUCH!
THERE'S ENOUGH THERE TO COVER EVERYONE'S DINNER TONIGHT.
SPLENDID!
GREAT COSTUMES, EVERYONE.
DINNER'S ON ME. HAPPY HALLOWEEN!
DINGG
WHEW!
YAAAY!

WHY'D YOU LET THEM GO?! THOSE WEREN'T KIDS IN THERE!
I KNOW.
THEN WHAT ARE WE GOING TO DO?
NOTHING.
THANKS FOR THE CALL.
QUITE THE TRICK THAT ALL THOSE VILLAINS ARE IN THERE TOGETHER.
BEFORE YOU ARREST THEM, GIVE THEM A MINUTE TO FINISH DINNER. MY TREAT.
HAPPY HALLOWEEN, KIDDIES! JOIN US IN THE NEXT CHAPTER FOR GOBBLES OF THANKSGIVING FUN IN BATMAN: LI'L GOTHAM!

THANKSGIVING

ON THIS SPECIAL DAY, LET US GIVE NO THANKS...
S
P

...TO THIS HOMICIDAL HOLIDAY THAT CELEBRATES THE MURDER AND CONSUMPTION OF OUR BRETHREN BIRDS.
ABSENT THEY SHALL FOREVER BE FROM THIS TABLE.

GOTHAM'S FEASTING WAYS. THIS VILE DAY OF OPPRESSION.
BUT LET US NOT WALLOW IN MISERY, OH NO! NOT WHEN WE CAN DO SOMETHING ABOUT IT.

PUT YOUR WINGS TOGETHER AND JOIN ME IN A TOAST, MY FEATHERED FRIENDS.
SQUAK!
LIVE FEED
SQUAK!
SQUAAK!
IT IS TIME... TO STAGE A MARCH OF THE TURKEYS!

WE ARE REPORTING LIVE DOWNTOWN ON MAIN STREET, AT THE ANNUAL GOTHAM THANKSGIVING PARADE.
THAT'S QUITE A CROWD IN ATTENDANCE! WOULDN'T YOU AGREE, VICKI?
ABSOLUTELY, JACK. IT'S A GOTHAM TRADITION! ONE THAT DATES BACK OVER SIXTY YEARS.
ALL OF THE FLOATS AND BALLOONS ARE SPONSORED BY LOCAL GOTHAM BUSINESSES. AND HERE COMES OUR FIRST ONE!
IT'S FUNDED FROM A PRIVATE DONATION. AND PROBABLY OUR MOST RECOGNIZABLE ONE IN THIS CITY...

...THE BATMAN!
LOOKS LIKE THE DARK KNIGHT GOT AN EARLY JUMP ON POTATOES AND STUFFING, VICKI.
HAW! FAT AND PATHETIC. YOU WASTED YOUR MONEY BUYING THAT.
QUITE THE CONTRARY. I'M SATISFIED.
WHY IS MY HEAD SO FAT?! AND BODY SO SMALL?!
TOTALLY UNREALISTIC.
TT... NOT EVEN THE RIGHT COSTUME. WHATEVER. HATE PARADES.
OUR FIRST FLOAT IS PROVIDED BY THE WAYNE FOUNDATION.
A TRADITIONAL MAYFLOWER SHIP, WHICH THE PILGRIMS USED TO--
BOOM
MY WORD!

THE MAYFLOWER HAS BEEN SUNK! OR RATHER EXPLODED.
VICKI, IS THAT--YES--IT APPEARS THAT PILGRIM IS A PENGUIN.
AND HE'S LEADING AN ARMY OF TURKEYS!
BE WARNED, GOTHAM. THESE BIRDS NO LONGER SHALL BE SHACKLED TO YOUR DINNER PLATES.
FEEL OUR TURKEY WRATH!
THAT'S JUST REVOLTING!
OR A REVOLT, VICKI.
TO THE BETTER PART OF THE MANSION!
THE BATCAVE.
THE BETTER-CAVE!

THE TIME IS AT HAND TO STEAL BACK THIS HOLIDAY FROM HUNGRY CONSUMERISM! HAVE YOUR DAY, MY FELLOW FLIGHTLESS FEATHERED FRIENDS!
WAAK WAK-- WHU?
IT'S OVER, COBBLEPOT! CONSIDER YOUR HOLIDAY PLANS CANCELED!
AND TAKE OFF THAT STUPID HAT!
BANGG
BANG
NEVER, YOU POINTY-EARED RODENT!
NO FUNNY LOOKING GUNS!
HA HA HA HA! QUIT IT!
WAAK!
PEK
PEK
PEK
I GOT'M, ROBIN! ROUND UP THE TURKEYS!
PEK PEK
PEK
O-HAHA KAY
HA!HA!

STOP PLAYING AROUND, ROBIN. STOP THE TURKEY MARCH!
GAWK!
OR JUST CONTINUE THE MARCH...!
GOOD WORK, ROBIN! LEAD THEM TO THE PETTING FARM AROUND THE CORNER!
GAH! THAT'S FOWL PLAY, BATMAN!

ALAS, I MUST GO ON LEAVE.
OR TAKE A HOLIDAY, IF YOU PREFER.
POK
FSSSH
SQUAK!
I GUESS FATMAN WAS SOME USE AFTER ALL!
DIDN'T KNOW YOU COULD PLAY THE TRUMPET, ROBIN.
THERE'S A LOT YOU DON'T KNOW ABOUT THE LEAGUE OF ASSASSINS... "DETECTIVE."
THIS BIRD JUST WASN'T MEANT TO FLY.
GOBBLE.

SLAP
OW! WHY'D YA SLAP ME, BABS?
IT'S "BARBARA." AND FIRST YOU MUST SAY GRACE.
GRACE?! YOU JUST SAID YOUR NAME WAS BARBARA!
OH, DAMIAN...
WHY MUST BERRIES BE IN SAUCE FORM?
I'M HAPPY YOU ALL COULD JOIN US TODAY.
EVERYTHING LOOKS AND SMELLS GREAT, ALFRED!
THANK YOU, MISS GORDON.
I'M SO HUNGRY I COULD EAT A PENGUIN.
EVERYONE HELP YOURSELVES.
WHERE'S MY SEAT? NO ONE EVER SAVES ME A SEAT.
WATCH YOUR BACK, SACRIFICIAL BIRD.
YOU STICK WITH ME, JERRY!
NIBBLE
NIBBLE
YES, I WONDER WHAT HAPPENED TO OUR ESTEEMED MR. COBBLEPOT. MASTER BRUCE?

"I'M SURE HE'S ENJOYING THE HOLIDAY JUST LIKE THE REST OF US.
"SURROUNDED BY FRIENDS."
CLANG CLANG CLANG
HEY, BIRDBRAIN. GET UP!
YER LUCKY YOU'RE HERE TODAY, OSWALD.
AND WHY'S THAT, YOU MISGUIDED MORON?

YOU MADE IT JUST IN TIME FOR DINNER!

WOULD YOU LIKE SOMETHING TO EAT, MR. SCARFACE?
I CAN'T EAT, YA DUMMY! BUT THAT BIG PALOOKA ALREADY HAS.
THAT'S NOT THE TRYPTOPHAN. MR. ZZZ JUST LIKES HIS NAPS.
ZZZ
HAPPY THANKSGIV
ZZZ
ITALY
REST THOSE WINGS AND TAKE A LOAD OFF.
I'M AFRAID THEY ALL STARTED WITHOUT YOU. BUT I MANAGED TO SNAG YOU A PLATE.
HOPE YOU LIKE TURKEY! I MEAN...WHO DOESN'T, RIGHT?
GOBBLE! GOBBLE!
HAPPY THANKSGIVING!
COME BACK FOR A LI'L HOLIDAY CHEER IN THE NEXT CHAPTER OF BATMAN: LI'L GOTHAM!

CHRISTMAS

THIS IS VICKI VALE, COMING TO YOU LIVE FROM GOTHAM PLAZA FOR THE ANNUAL LIGHTING OF THE CHRISTMAS TREE.
THE MAYOR IS ABOUT TO ADDRESS THE CROWD. LET'S LISTEN.
WE ARE PLEASED YOU ALL COULD JOIN US FOR THIS MOMENTOUS OCCASION, EVEN IN THIS WEATHER. GOOD WILL AND PEACE TO ALL.
NORMALLY OUR CHOIR WOULD HAVE SOME CAROLS TO SING YOU. BUT APPARENTLY THEY TOOK A SNOW DAY AS WELL.
CARE TO BELT OUT A TUNE, COMMISSIONER?
HAHAHAHAHAHA!
VERY WELL. LET'S NOT WASTE ANY MORE TIME. YOU CAME HERE FOR LIGHTS. LET'S GIVE YOU LIGHTS.
CLICK
OOOOOOOOOOOH!

DO YOU TAKE SONG REQUESTS? I WAS HOPING FOR A RUDOLPH MEDLEY.
NOT ON MY SALARY.
THE CITY OWES YOU A DEBT OF THANKS FOR SPONSORING THIS EVENT, BRUCE.
IT'S MY PLEASURE, JIM. ALWAYS HAPPY TO HELP.
AND WHERE'S YOUNG DAMIAN TONIGHT? I FIGURE HE WOULD LOVE TO COME OUT AND HECKLE AT GOTHAM'S FINEST.
OH, HE'S HELPING ALFRED GET THE PLACE ALL DECORATED FOR THE SEASON.
"THEY BOTH COULD USE THE BONDING TIME."
I WONDER WHAT HAPPENED TO THE CHILDREN'S CHOIR? THEY'VE NEVER MISSED THIS EVENT BEFORE.
IN THIS WEATHER, I HOPE THEY DIDN'T GET INTO AN ACCIDENT. RIGHT, WAYNE... *WAYNE?*
NOW, WHERE DID HE RUN OFF TO?
HMPH! TALKING TO MYSELF IS BECOMING A HABIT.
WAIT--I'VE GOT IT! WHY DIDN'T I SEE THIS BEFORE? BRUCE WAYNE'S TRUE IDENTITY IS...

"...SANTA CLAUS!"
HO HO HOOOOOO!
ALFRED, DO YOU REMEMBER THE NAME OF THE ORPHANAGE THAT SINGS FOR THE TREE LIGHTING CEREMONY?
SKREEEECH
THAT WOULD BE SAINT PETER'S ACADEMY. ARE YOU GENTLEMEN LOOKING TO ENROLL? IT'S NEVER TOO LATE TO LEARN MANNERS AND PROPER ETIQUETTE...FOR ANY OF YOU.
THAT'S WHAT I PAY YOU FOR.
HANDSOMELY, SIR.
I'M PULLING UP THEIR BUS ROUTE ON MY NAVIGATION MAPS.
I BELIEVE WE'VE FOUND THEM.

THE BUS APPEARS TO HAVE LOST CONTROL OVER THE ICY ROADS.
OR MAYBE SOMEONE ELSE WAS TO BLAME.
HHH-HHH-HELP UUU-UUU-US...
REMAIN CALM. I'M GOING TO MELT THE ICE.
BZZT
YOU'RE SAFE HERE. STAY AND GET WARM.
THH-THANK YOU, BATMAN. HE WENT THAT WAY.
PLEASE, HHH-HURRY!
THERE! A SNOW-GLOBE...? FREEZE!

LET THE CHILDREN GO, VICTOR... NOW!
THEY ARE NOT MY PRISONERS, BATMAN. EACH CHILD IS LIKE A SNOWFLAKE--INDIVIDUAL. UNIQUE. PRECIOUS.
AND SO VERY FRAGILE.
IT IS MY INTENTION TO KEEP THEM SAFE FROM THE HARSHNESS AND CRUELNESS OF GOTHAM CITY. TO PROVIDE THESE ORPHANS A NURTURING HOME INSTEAD OF BEING EXPLOITED IN YOUR RITUALISTIC HOLIDAY EVENTS.
THEY WILL RETURN WITH ME, AND TOGETHER, WE WILL LIVE AND FLOURISH IN SECLUSION FROM THE EVILS OF THIS WORLD.
I AM THEIR GUARDIAN. THEIR PROTECTOR.
THEIR CAPTOR!
IF YOU WON'T RELEASE THEM, VICTOR, THEN I WILL.

YOU ARE WELCOME TO FAIL. BOTH OF YOU.
KRIIKOOOM
THE CHILL HAS AFFECTED YOUR AIM, BATMAN.
ONLY IF I HAD AIMED FOR YOUR GUN.
FZZZ
YOU KIDS ALL RIGHT IN THERE?
WE'RE OKAY. RAN OUTTA POPCORN THOUGH.
LET THE CHILDREN GO, VICTOR. YOU CAN DO MORE GOOD IN OTHER WAYS.
WHY, I CAN THINK OF A FEW YOU'D BE TERRIFIC AT...

GOTHAM CITY BLADES
HALY'S winter CIRCUS
"YOU CAN BE MR. ZAMBONI FOR THE GOTHAM BLADES.
GOTHAM CITY BLADES
"I HEAR HALY'S WINTER CIRCUS NEEDS A POLAR BEAR WRANGLER.
"HECK, I BET YOU'D MAKE A MEAN ICE CREAM!
"I DON'T MEAN YOU'RE MEAN... JUST THAT... YOU GET MY POINT."
ICE CREAM?! I WANT ICE CREAM!!
WHAT? NO! TOO MANY VOICES... STOP. PLEASE, STOP!!
EVERY KID NEEDS TO BE HEARD. EVERY ONE GIVEN THEIR OWN PERSONAL ATTENTION. TO BE LOVED AND PROTECTED.
THAT IS THE JOB OF A PARENT.
AND EVERY KID DESERVES PARENTS.

...
WE DO NOT SHARE THE SAME PHILOSOPHY, BATMAN, BUT I FEEL WE SHARE THE SAME GOAL.
KIDS, STEP AWAY FROM THE ICE AND I'LL GET YOU OUT.
WAIT! THERE'S A DOOR ON THE OTHER SIDE.
THAT'S HOW I GOT HIM OUT. IT WASN'T LOCKED. EVEN HAS A COOL ICE SLIDE ATTACHED.
I LIKE SLIDES...
YOU'RE FREE. NOW SLOWLY AND CAREFULLY...
HEY MISTER, YOU WANNA COME HANG OUT WITH US? WE'RE GONNA GO SING SOME SONGS TONIGHT. IT'LL BE FUN.
NO, CHILD. I DO NOT SING.
WELL, MAYBE NEXT YEAR THEN, HUH?

Arkham Asylum.
Jingle bell, Batman fell, right into the ice...
...Santa's list, I was missed, am naughty never niiiice!
Haaaaiii, caaarrrlll...
H-H-H-Hullo... Miss Isley... M-M-Merry C-C-Christmas...
You hear he just turned himself in? No struggle almost.
Really?
Yup. I mean... why not? Not like he has anyone to go home to. Poor guy.
Siiiilent niiiight...
...Hoooly niiiight...

...ALL IS CALM...
...ALL IS BRIGHT...
...SLEEP IN HEAVENLY PEACE...
FROM: Sarah, Saida, Derek, & Dustin
TO: The Fans

NEW YEAR'S EVE

GIVE SOME THOUGHT TO WHAT WE TALKED ABOUT, SELINA.
I'LL SLEEP ON IT, BATS.
58763876376B
27687686787
GOOD, SHE'S ALONE.
OKAY, LET'S GO.

MRRoW
MEW
MEW
I GET IT. YOU'RE HUNGRY...
MEW
...ALL OF YOU. WE ALL WANT SOMETHING.
EVEN HIM.
MEW
I KNOW, SAMMY. HE HAS THE BEST OF INTENTIONS. WE'LL TURN OVER A NEW LEAF THIS YEAR.
CREEK
SHHH...
FUMPH
HAPPY NEW YEAR!
OH, NO...
PUH-LEEEEZE, SELINA, LET'S DO SOMETHING TO CELEBRATE! I'VE BEEN SO BORED SINCE BATSY DRAGGED MISTAH J BACK TO THE PEN. LET ME HAVE SOME FUN!
OHHHH, NO! NOT AGAIN. I'M CHANGING MY WAYS FOR GOOD THIS YEAR. AND THERE'S NOTHING THE TWO OF YOU CAN SAY. REMEMBER WHAT HAPPENED LAST NEW YEAR?
SELINA, WE'LL MAKE IT FOR A GOOD CAUSE...FOR THE PLANET, THE CHILDREN, THE ANIMALS. ALL THE STUFF THAT YOU LOVE. COME ON, GIRL!
WELL... IF IT'S FOR A GOOD CAUSE...

ALL RIGHT, GIRLS, LET'S MAKE THIS A...
...NEW YEAR'S REVOLUTION!
THANKS FOR JOINING US, SELINA! YOU WON'T REGRET IT.
THAT REMAINS TO BE SEEN.
BOINGY BOINGY!!
BOINGE BOINGE
YOU REALLY DON'T HAVE TO MAKE THAT SOUND.
I DON'T HAVE TO, BUT I'M GONNA.
IT'S GOING TO BE A LONG NIGHT.
BOINGE
BOINGY!

ARDORA COSMETICS
THEIR CEO GOES BY THE NAME OF "FERVOR." HER COMPANY IS A DETRIMENT TO THE ENVIRONMENT.
CHEATING THEIR WAY THROUGH EVERY EPA REGULATION TO PRODUCE THEIR DAMAGING PRODUCTS. THEY CONTINUE TO PUMP TOXINS INTO OUR AIR AND WATER. *BUT NO MORE!*
IT'S ABOUT TO GET REALLY BEAUTIFUL UP IN HERE, LADIES.
BOOOM
WOOHOOO! MAXIMUM FERVOCITY!!
CLANGG
WELL, SAVING THE ENVIRONMENT ISN'T BAD.

YAYYYYY!
GAMES
TOYS
HARLEY! I THOUGHT I TOLD YOU... NEW WAYS! CHANGE! NO MORE TROUBLES! ALL THAT!!
BUT THE KIDS BACK AT THE ORPHANAGE WHO NEVER GET THE GOOD TOYS WILL LOVE THESE!
BLOCKS
PUZZLES
THINK ABOUT THE CHILDREN, SELINA.
WON'T SOMEONE THINK OF THE CHILDREN?
YEAH, S'LINA! THINK ABOUT THE KIDDIES--OH, AND HANG ON TIGHT.
FOR THE CHILDREN!!
GOTHAM CITY Gallery
HONK HONK
KRASSSHHHH
OF COURSE... THE CHILDREN. THAT'S ALWAYS A GOOD THING.

SHHHH... BE VERY VERY QUIET...
BARK BARK
FILTHY ANIMALS!
RUF RUFF
WHAT?!
THE PEOPLE WHO DID THIS, HARL. THEY DISGUST ME!
MEEOOOW
CLICK
GIGGLE!
AWW... THIS LOOKS LIKE ONE A MY BAY-BEEES.
CAN WE KEEP HIM?
NO! BUT THAT DOESN'T MEAN "THEY" GET TO, EITHER.
AWW, DON'TCHU WORRY ABOUT THEM! YOU AND YOUR PALS CAN STAY AT AUNTIE HARLEY AND UNCLE J'S WHILE HE'S AWAY!
...FOR THE ANIMALS. DEFINITELY!

THIS IS EGG-CITING!
TIME TO HAM IT UP!
SMOOTH, HARL.
I'M ALL FOR BREAKING AND ENTERING--
AND TAKING!!
--BUT REMIND ME WHY WE'RE HERE AGAIN?
KRASSHH
!?
THIS GUY ONCE KICKED ME OUT OF HIS LAME-O NIGHTCLUB FOR "IMPROPER ATTIRE."
HE SAID THIS WAS NOT THE PROPER HEADWEAR FOR A BLACK AND WHITE THEMED EVENT. CAN YOU BELIEVE THAT?! THE NERVE...
COBBLEPOT
"THAT STOOPID RUINED MY CUPID. WRECKED MY VALENTINE'S DATE WITH MY PUDDIN'.
WHEEEEE!
WELL, HERE'S "EGG" ON HIS FACE. OR IN MY HAND. HAH!
I GUESS IT'S OKAY, IF IT'S FOR... LOVE?

MMMMMMM!
CHOCOLATE-CARAMEL-COCONUT--
I LOVE THEIR GLUTEN-FREE TRIPLE VANILLA FUDGE CUPCAKES!
BESTEST... LOLLIPOPS... IN... THE... WHOLE...
ZZZZZZ
YOU KNOW WHAT THEY SAY, RED...
I CAN'T STAND IT ANYMORE!! ARGHH!
OH, NO... NO NO NO...
IN CASE OF EMERGENCY... BREAK GLASS!!
SPLURT
HOORAY FOR TEAMWORK!!
I GUESS IT'S OKAY, IF IT'S FOR... CANDY...?
RITS ROKAY ROR RANDY NOM NOM NOM.
HOORAY.

THE NIGHT IS YOUNG. WHAT'S NEXT? THE ZOO? THE AQUARIUM??
OH! OH! THE CIRCUS!
AND RIDE ALL THE ANIMALS AND TEACH THEM TO DANCE!
NO, HARL... THAT'S NOT REVOLUTIONARY AT ALL. WE HAVE TO BE CONCISE IN OUR ACTIONS. DO IT FOR A CAUSE. MAKE A DIFFERENCE IN THE WORLD!
I SAY WE BREAK INTO THE DOWNTOWN GOTHAM ATRIUM, TAKE OUT ALL THE GUARDS, FORCE OUR WAY PAST THE CARETAKERS AND MAINTENANCE PERSONNEL... AND THEN...
...WE WATER ALL THE PLANTS!
PRETTY REVOLUTIONARY THERE, "CHE."
WHAT?! IT'LL BE FUN, TOO!
I KNOW, I KNOW!! WE CAN GO ROB THAT GOODY-GOODY BRUCE WAYNE AGAIN! I KNOW WHERE HE KEEPS ALL HIS FAVORITE RIDES.
OR... WE CAN GO SHOPPING.
FOR SHOES--AND FANCY HATS. MAYBE EVEN... ICE CREAM?

AND SO...
HMMM... NOT BAD.
~YAWN~ YEE-HAW!
A ONE AND A TWO...
VERY BAD. STRIKE A POSE, GIRLS.
ARE WE DONE YET?
MEW
WE'VE BARELY STARTED. WE STILL HAVE THE GOTHAM BOTANICAL GARDENS AND THE ARBORETUM.
LEAD THE WAY, SAMMY.
HEY, SELINA. SO I REWORKED THE CATAPULT TO CLEAR THE NORTH ARKHAM WALL IF--
WHOA! YOU JERKS THREW A PARTY? WHY WASN'T I INVITED?
AWW... YER KISSES ARE SWEET, MISTAH J... ZZZZZ
OH, WELL. NEXT YEAR, FOR SURE. A DEFINITE NEW YEAR'S RESOLUTION--
--REVOLUTION!
THIS MESS IS GOING TO TAKE A WHILE TO CLEAN UP, BUT JOIN US AGAIN FOR THE NEXT CHAPTER OF BATMAN: LI'L GOTHAM!

VALENTINE'S DAY

THIS IS MY D-DAY. THE DAY THAT I DREAD.
IT'S WORSE THAN CAPTURE. WORSE THAN ARKHAM.
EVEN WORSE THAN BATMAN TRIUMPHANT...
FTTT
SORRY, MISTAH J...

"...IT'S SPENDING THE DAY AS HARLEY'S LOVE PRISONER."
...I WAS ONLY AIMING FOR YOUR HEART.
AROOO?
SIGH

AWWW. DON'T BE STUPID, COME 'ERE TO CUPID!
WHAT'SA MATTER, PUDDIN'?
POP
SORRY, MY DEAR. GONNA HAVE TO TAKE A RAINCHECK ON THAT ONE. CRIME'S A CALLIN'... MAYBE I'LL PICK SOMETHING UP FOR YOU.
POP
THIS IS THE WORST HA-HA-HOLIDAY EVER. IF ONLY I COULD SHARE MY MISERY...
...ACTUALLY CHOOSE WHO LOVES WHOM ON THIS DAY. THEN THE JOKE WOULD BE ON EVERYONE ELSE. YEAH!
"AND I'VE GOT JUST THE WAY TO DO IT.
POISON IVY'S GOT A POTION HERE FOR EVERYTHING.
SNIFF SNIFF
HMMM... NOW, WHICH ONE OF THESE WILL DO THE TRICK?

YOU!
HOW DARE YOU BREAK INTO MY GREENHOUSE...
SPLASH
..."MISTAH J"...
WHAAA--?
...THE AROMA...THE SCENT...
...IT MAKES YOU... IRRESISTIBLE!
GAH! GET THEM OFF ME!
DOWN, BOY!
CHOMP
OH BOY, WAIT 'TIL HARL GETS A LOAD OF THIS!
KRASHH

THAT GIRL REALLY *IS* POISON! AND WHAT IS THIS SMELL?! GOTTA WASH THIS REEK OFF ME!
SCREECH
I'VE BEEN A FOOL. BUT HARLEY WON'T BE *TOO* UPSET.
I JUST NEED TO BRING HER SOMETHING TO SMOOTH THINGS OVER--
THIS'LL DO. MY KINDA "KITTY LITTER!"
THANKS FOR CATCHIN' THAT FOR ME, MR. 'KER...
MMM... OL' HARL WAS RIGHT. YOU'RE NOT A BAD CATCH YERSELF. PRRR
HEY-- HEY!
GETOFFAHMEE!
WELL, AT LEAST DIAMOND'S ARE FOREVER.
MEW MEW

OKAY...IT CAN'T BE COINCIDENCE THAT TWO FEMME FATALES HAVE FALLEN FOR ME.
AND THIS STENCH MAKES IT HARD TO NOT GET NOTICED.
THE GREEN HAIR AND PURPLE SUIT DOESN'T HELP EITHER, CLOWN.
I NEED A DISGUISE...
HEY!
YOINK
COOCHIE COOCHIE COO... GOO GOO, NO POO POO!
I'M NOT A BABY, YOU--
--HANDSOME FREAK...!
AYAAA... I'VE BEEN ROBBED!
AND I'VE BEEN ROBED. HEE HEE!
THAT SMELL...
GAAAAH!
DON'T RUN AWAY!
IT'S TIME TO BE LOVED, MY BELOVED!

THE NEWS IS RIGHT, FOR A CHANGE. THE STREETS OF GOTHAM *ARE* DANGEROUS.
I'M BETTER OFF IN HERE.
BEEEELOVED!
LAZARUS PITS REALLY DO MAKE PEOPLE CRAZY.
OHHH, NOOOO... I AM IN THE *WRONG* PLACE.
WELCOME, MY LOVE.
OR THE RIGHT ONE. DO YOU BELIEVE IN MAGIC?
UHH... NO?
THEN WHY ARE YOU WEARING A LOVE POTION?
ON EPACSE
SSIK SSIK
SEND OUT THE CLOWN!
SEND OUT THE CLOWN!

OPEN SESAME!
PAK
BOOM
AWWW! NOW YOU SEE HIM...
SHOOOOMM
...NOW YOU DON'T. HEHEHEHEHH.
I WANT TO THANK YOU-- ERRR--
THEY CALL ME ROXY.
AND THE PLEASURE...IS ALL MINE.
WHERE...UM... WHERE ARE WE GOING?
SKY'S THE LIMIT, BABE.
TOTALLY WORTH ITTTT
ANOTHER LOVE LOST TO MID-AIR EVASION. TWICE TODAY.

HARLEY?!
WELL, LOOK WHO DECIDED TO COME FALLIN' BACK!
MMM... AND I AM SOOOOOOO GLAD TO SEE YOU, MISTAH J...
I'M SO GLAD TO SEE YOU! YOU HAVE NO IDEA.
WAIT, HARL-- WAIT-!
COME 'ERE, PUDDIN'!
SCREEEEC
CCHH
WHAT'S THE MATTA, LOU? WHO'S FOLLOWING US?
AROO
WHAT DO YOU MEAN, "ALL OF THEM?!"
MAKE IT STOP! PLEEEEZE, MAKE IT STOP!!

JUST A BUNCHA SUPER DUDES, HANGIN' OUT... IN SPACE, PUTTING UP SOME SORTA SUPER SATELLITE...
SEE, GUYS? THIS IS WHAT I'M TALKIN' ABOUT!
NO FLOWERS TO PICK UP.
NO DINNER RESERVATIONS TO MAKE.
NO LAST MINUTE SHOPPING.
NO KIDDING.
AHEM
AHEM GETTING A DISTRESS CALL FROM GOTHAM... YOUR PAL JOKER'S ON A RAMPAGE.
GOTHAM NEEDS MY HELP!
NO... JUST THE JOKER, ACTUALLY. TO ESCAPE FROM EVERY WOMAN IN GOTHAM.
STORY OF MY LIFE.
LET'S GET THE OTHER SIDE OF THIS AIRLOCK MODULE INSTALLED, PUT UP THE LEFT SOLAR PANEL, THEN GO FOR SOME BURGERS.
SEE? THIS IS WHAT I'M TALKIN' ABOUT!
YOU GUYS WOULD NOT BELIEVE HOW MANY TIMES I'M EXPECTED TO PRESENT A RING-- EVERY YEAR!
WELL, ONCE THEY KNOW YOU CAN MAKE DIAMONDS OUT OF COALS IN YOUR HANDS, THE MAGIC'S GONE.
SHOW OFF.
NO! YOU CAN ONLY RESORT TO THAT SO MANY TIMES IS WHAT I'M SAYING.
SHOW OFF.
"I'LL CALL THE BIRDS ON THIS."
HUNTRESS, REPORT.
IT APPEARS JOKER SPRAYED HIMSELF WITH SOME TYPE OF PHEROMONE FROM POISON IVY.
I JUST FOUND THE ANTIDOTE.
HAVE YOU FOUND THE JOKER?
I DON'T THINK THAT'S GOING TO BE A PROBLEM.

HOPE I'M NOT TOO LATE. HE'S GOT TO BE UNDER THERE SOMEWHERE, RIGHT?
SSSSSCHHHHH
THE HORROR... THE HORROR.
I'LL SHOW YOU "HORROR!"
SAVE MEEEE!
SORRY. THERE'S NO ANTIDOTE FROM A SCORNED WOMAN.
HAPPY VALENTINE'S DAY... I GUESS.
THIS. IS A. DISGUSTING. HOLIDAY.
COME BACK FOR A NEW CHAPTER OF BATMAN: LI'L GOTHAM, WITH MORE ME IN IT.

LUNAR NEW YEAR

WHY DOES THIS ALWAYS HAPPEN?
WHAT'S MORE IMPORTANT THAN TRAINING? WHERE IS HE?
MASTER BRUCE IS RATHER BUSY AT THE MOMENT.
I JUST KNOW HE DITCHED ME TO GO BEAT DOWN THUGS, ALL BY HIMSELF!
HE KNOWS HOW MUCH I LIKE TO DO THAT, TOO...
"BET HE'S FIGHTING A BUNCHA CLOWNS. *OOOH!* PROBABLY MUD MEN, RIGHT? OR EVEN SOLVING RIDDLES."
MUCH WORSE, I'M AFRAID...
"...A MEETING WITH THE BOARD OF DIRECTORS!"
AND I'M STUCK WITH YOU. I DON'T NEED TO BE BABYSAT!
IS THAT HOW YOU SEE ME?
BABYSITTER, NURSEMAID, LACKEY, ***BUTLER***... ALL THE SAME. WHAT ELSE IS THERE TO SEE?
YOU'VE BARELY SCRATCHED THE SURFACE, MASTER DAMIAN.
HEHE... ***BUTT***-LER.

ROAR
GAH!
WHAT ARE WE DOING HERE?
TO CONTINUE YOUR TRAINING.
AHH... DIM SUM, AND THEN SOME.
I'D RATHER TRAIN WITH MY FATHER.
AND WHERE DO YOU THINK HE TRAINED?
I ALWAYS JUST ASSUMED HE WAS BORN IN THAT CAVE, TRAINED BY...BAT...MEN?
CLANG
CLANG

GREETINGS, OLD FRIEND. PLEASE, COME INSIDE.
HEY, DAMIAN.
I CALLED MISS KATANA TO JOIN US TODAY. THE TWO OF YOU WILL BE TRAINING TOGETHER.
AWW, MAN-- WHAT?! I'M NOT PRACTICING WITH A GIRL!
WHY NOT? I AM.
I HOPE YOU'VE BEEN PRACTICING, 'CUZ I'M GONNA WHOOP YOUR SPOILED. LITTLE. BUTT.
GULP

MY WORD! WHAT HAPPENED HERE?
THERE WAS A BREAK-IN AT OUR SCHOOL EARLIER THIS MORNING.
SO I GUESS THIS MEANS NO TRAINING TODAY.
YOUR LUCKY DAY, HUH?
PLEASE.

MUCH DAMAGE. BUT ONLY ONE ITEM WAS TAKEN.
THE BLADE OF THE JADE SERPENT.

AND YOU KNOW THIS, HOW?

I WAS THERE THE FIRST TIME IT WAS TAKEN.

"BACK WHEN YOUR FATHER WAS FIRST PLAYING DRESS UP, HE DIDN'T HAVE A ROBIN. ANY OF THEM.
"BUT THAT DOESN'T MEAN HE DIDN'T HAVE A PARTNER."
WHERE TO, MASTER BATMAN?
JUST BATMAN, ALFRED. AND WE'RE GOING TO THE GOTHAM HISTORICAL MUSEUM.
TAKING IN A LATE NIGHT EXHIBIT, SIR?
YOU MIGHT SAY THAT. BEFORE SOMEONE ELSE TAKES IT.
VROOOOM
QUIT FUSSING WITH YOUR MASK. YOU HAVE TO DRESS THE PART IF YOU'RE OUT WITH ME TONIGHT.
GROAN
THE THINGS I DO FOR THE WAYNE FAMILY. I LOOK FORWARD TO THE DAY YOU GET YOUR OWN VEHICLE.
AND YOUR OWN SIDEKICK.
HALEY'S CIRCUS
FLYING GRAYSONS

"THE MUSEUM'S EXHIBIT OF ANCIENT WEAPONRY CAUGHT OUR ATTENTION. AND WE WEREN'T THE ONLY ONES."
GOTHAM
WEAPONRY
KRASHHH
RA'S AL GHUL!
GREETINGS, DETECTIVE.
I WON'T ALLOW YOU TO TAKE THAT!
I'M NOT HERE TO STEAL THE SWORD, BUT TO PROTECT IT. AS A FAVOR TO A FRIEND.
I'M AFRAID YOU HAVE ME MISTAKEN...
...FOR THEM!
KOBRAAAAAAA!
"WE FOUGHT OFF THE KOBRA CULT, BUT THEIR LEADER WAS ABLE TO TAKE THE SWORD DURING THE COMMOTION.
EXIT

"WE TRAVELED THE WORLD, SEEKING WHERE SNAKES DWELL. AND WE FOUGHT THEM IN THEIR SECRET BASE.
"ONCE WE RECOVERED THE SWORD, THE MUSEUM HAD IT RETURNED TO ITS ORIGINAL OWNER."
MANY YEARS HAVE PASSED. THE SWORD IS LOST ONCE MORE...FOR THE LAST TIME, I FEAR.
NEVER!
I HAVE ONLY TO CALL A *FAMILY FRIEND* TO HELP US SEARCH.
I'M AFRAID HE'S STILL STUCK IN A CLOSED-DOOR MEETING, MR. PENNYWORTH. I'M TO HOLD ALL HIS CALLS.
OH, DEAR. IT SEEMS HE'S UNAVAILABLE AT THE MOMENT.
BREW UP SOME OOLONG TEA.
...OR WHATEVER KINDA LEAF JUICE YOU OLD GUYS DRINK.
WE WON'T BE GONE LONG.

THESE STREETS ARE PACKED! WHY'S IT SO BUSY?
IT'S LUNAR NEW YEAR, SILLY... CHINESE NEW YEAR? TET? SEOLLAL? IT'S "THE YEAR OF THE SNAKE" THIS YEAR.
UGH, SNAKES.
YOU SEE THAT? WHY DO SNAKES NEED JEWELRY?
TO RING IN THE NEW YEAR?
OKAY, I'M IGNORING YOU NOW.
HEY, WAIT UP!
THEY'RE ALL GOING DOWN THERE.
UUUGH, MAN, SEWERS?! GROSS!
QUIT YOUR WHINING, PRINCESS, AND GET YOUR BIG HEAD IN THERE.
LOOK, HE HAS THE JADE SWORD!
NOT FOR LONG.
FORK IT OVER, KOBRA KING!
FOOLISH CHILDREN. THAT SSSWORD IS NO MATCH. AND NEITHER ARE YOU.
THIS SSSTINKS!
STOP.

YEP, IT DEFINITELY SSSTINKS TO BE US.
WILL YOU QUIT THAT, AND START THINKING OF A WAY OUT OF HERE.
NOW WHAT ARE YOU DOING?
CHECK IT-- I DID THIS WITH TURKEYS ONCE... MAYBE WE CAN GET RID OF THE SNAKES LIKE A PIED PIPER.
HE USED A FLUTE TO LURE CHILDREN AND RATS, NOT SNAKES.
HMM... THEN MAYBE THE RATS WILL EAT THE SNAKES.
YOU'VE REALLY GOT NO CONCEPT OF REALITY.
BUT AT THIS POINT, ANY HELP WOULD BE APPRECIATED.
"YOU'RE A FORTUNE COOKIE. I THINK YOU GOT YOUR WISH!
I CAN'T WATCH.
THEY DON'T STAND A CHANCE. THEY DON'T EVEN SEE THAT SNAKE.
THEN YOU'RE MISSING OUT!
CHAACK

YEAH! GO OLD SCHOOL! REALLY OLD!
SMACK
BAM
SO THE SNAKE HAS SPROUTED LEGS.
I'LL NEVER SSSURRENDER!
HERE, DAMIAN. I GOT SOMETHING FOR YOU: ANOTHER PET.
BLEH!
I LIKE ANIMALS. BUT I DRAW THE LINE AT SNAKES.
ARE YOU TWO ALL RIGHT?
THAT WAS SOOOO COOL!
I'LL TAKE THAT AS A YES.

YOU'RE LATE.
I HAD BUSINESS. STOCK BUSINESS.
WHATEVS. YOU WEREN'T EVEN NEEDED.
SO YOU WERE ABLE TO HANDLE THINGS, DAMIAN?
ACTUALLY... EVEN I WASN'T NEEDED, IF YOU CAN BELIEVE THAT. YOUR BUTLER SAVED THE DAY.
YOU REALLY LIKE SAYING THAT WORD.
FROM THE MOUTHS OF BABES. THE YOUNG MASTER EXAGGERATES. I HAD HELP.
YOU SHOULDA SEEN THEM.
BIFF! BAM! POW!
HI-YA!
MY FAMILY KICKS BUTT! EVEN YOU, ALFRED.
OF COURSE, BECAUSE HE'S...
...THE BUTT-LER!!
QUITE THE...RINGING ENDORSEMENT.
NEXT TIME, YOU STAY HOME AND CLEAN THAT GIANT PENNY. ALFRED AND I ARE GOING OUT ON PATROL.
TOSS ME THE KEYS, ALF. THIS TIME, I'M DRIVING YOU HOME.
OH, DEAR. I THINK NOT.
FAITH AND BEGORRAH! JOIN US FOR THE NEXT CHAPTER OF BATMAN: LI'L GOTHAM, AS THE CITY GOES GREEN WITH MISCHIEF!

SAINT PATRICK'S DAY

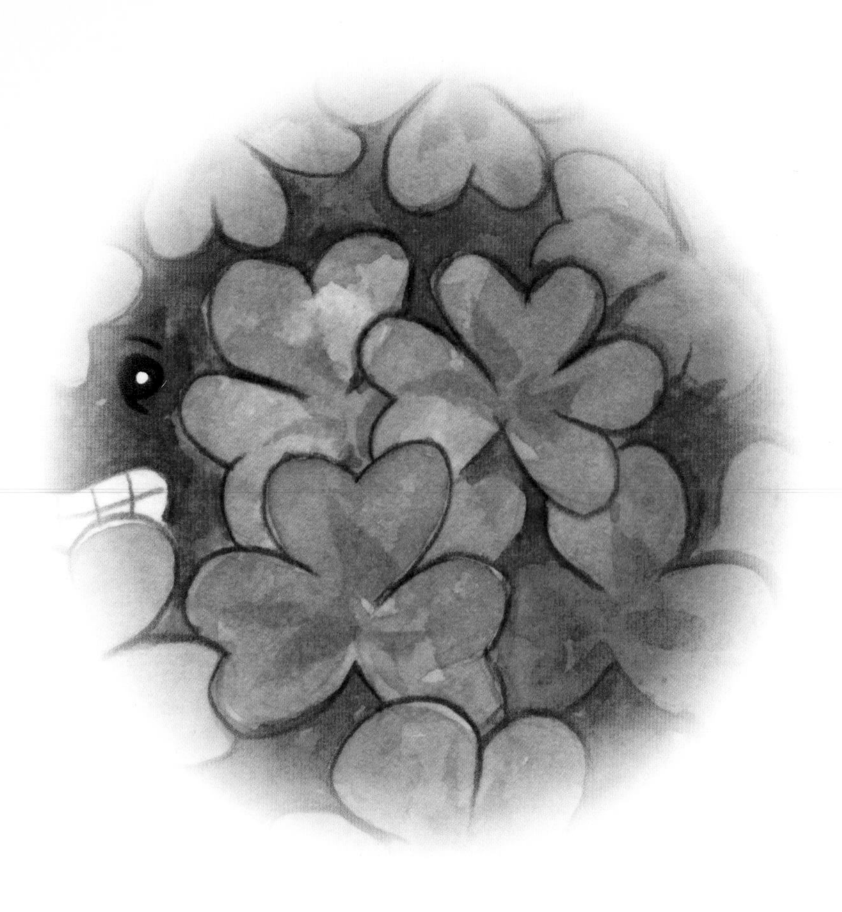

DON'TCHA FEEL LEFT OUT, COMMISH?
THE PARTY IS GOING ON OUT THERE AND WE'RE STUCK IN HERE.
WHAT DO YOU MEAN?
I DON'T DO THIS FOR FUN. OUR JOBS ARE EXCITING ENOUGH.
AND RELAX, HARVEY. GO HELP YOURSELF TO A DONUT.
ARGH!
WHY CAN'T THEY MAKE NORMAL DONUTS? WHO LIKES A GREEN DONUT?!
RRRNG
A GREEN BEAR CLAW?! SINCE WHEN ARE BEARS GREEN?!
WHO SAID IT WAS A BEAR?
YOU'RE GOING TO HAVE TO SPEAK UP, CADET. WHAT'S THE PROBLEM?
YOU'RE NEEDED AT THE GOTHAM COUNTY BANK & TRUST. IT'S BEEN ROBBED.
BULLOCK, LET'S GO! WE'RE ON CALL.
MMMM... GREEN'S MY FAVORITE COLOR.

BY THE TIME THE MANAGER GOT HERE, THE VAULT WAS EMPTY. CLEANED OUT.
SECURITY CAMERAS?
DIDN'T FILM ANYTHING, SIR. THERE WAS ONE ODD THING LEFT BEHIND, THOUGH.
I THINK WE'VE GOT OUR PRIME SUSPECT, COMMISH... LITTLE GREEN MEN.
CLEAR THE ROOM, EVERYONE. LET'S GIVE HIM SPACE TO WORK.
THAT INCLUDES YOU, TOO, BULLOCK.
SHEESH... GIVING ME THE SHAMROCK SHAKEDOWN.
LEPRECHAUNS?
IN THIS TOWN, ANYTHING IS POSSIBLE.

LOOKS PRETTY CLEAN.
LOOKS CAN BE DECEIVING.

WE HAVEN'T HAD A CHANCE TO DUST FOR PRINTS.
THEN I'LL TAKE A CLOSER LOOK. HIT THE LIGHTS.
FSSSHT

CATWOMAN! OF COURSE.

I'M BACK, MY BABIES. DID YOU MISS ME?
MEW
MEW
MEW
YOU KNOW, BREAKING AND ENTERING IS A CRIME.
SO IS BANK ROBBERY.
I HAVE NO IDEA WHAT YOU'RE TALKING ABOUT.
BUT SINCE YOUR CLAWS ARE OUT, THEN SO ARE MINE.
SELINA--
--JUST...
...GIVE ME...
...THE *BAG.*

OOF!
HEY, WHAT ARE YOU DOING? WE'RE FIGHTIN' HERE!
CAT FOOD?! WHERE'S THE MONEY FROM THE BANK?
I TOLD YOU, I DIDN'T STEAL ANYTHING. EVEN GOT A RECEIPT FOR THE KITTY CHOW.
DON'T YOU TRUST ME?
CLANK
I TRUST THE LAW WILL SORT THIS OUT.
I HAD NO IDEA THE BATMOBILE HAD A BACK SEAT.
NOT BAD. PRETTY ROOMY!
BATMAN! THERE'S BEEN A HEIST AT THE SECOND NATIONAL BANK.
DID YOU FIND ANYTHING?
YOU'LL NEVER GUESS. A SHAMROCK! ALSO ONE OTHER THING...
I ALREADY HAVE A HUNCH WHAT THE SECOND ITEM IS--A COIN?

YOUR KIND ISN'T ALLOWED HERE.
HEROES?
NO... YOU'RE NOT TWINS.
HAVEN'T YOU HEARD OF THE DYNAMIC DUO BEFORE?
DOUBLE INDEMNITY SECURITY
KRAAK
DON'T BOTHER. THEY AIN'T HIRING.
FRAGGIN' WASTE A' MY TIME.
YOU KNOW WHY I'M HERE, HARVEY.
I RUN A LEGIT BUSINESS. "TWICE THE PROTECTION AT TWICE THE PRICE."
NEXT TIME YOU HIT A BANK, MAKE SURE IT DOESN'T HAVE "SECOND" IN THE TITLE.
OR LEAVE BEHIND ANY EVIDENCE.
TOO BAD THAT'S NOT MINE.
BUT IF YOU WANT, WE CAN FLIP FOR IT.
I WIN.
BEST TWO OUT OF THREE?
HEY, IS THAT A BACK SEAT IN YOUR CAR?

ONE ROOFTOP MEETING LATER...
WHICH ONE IS IT THIS TIME?
THE CENTRAL BANK OF GOTHAM. SAME VARIATION OF CLUES.
AND I'VE ALREADY DISPATCHED MY MEN TO GRAB OUR PRIME SUSPECT.

AGGH!
IT'S THE FUZZ!
DON'T SHOOT! JUST US CLOWNS...ERR... CLOWNING AROUND.

WE'RE YOUR FRIENDLY NEIGHBORHOOD LOST & FOUND. JUST RETURNING A CARD YOU LEFT BEHIND IN THE VAULT YOU STOLE FROM, ALONG WITH A SHAMROCK.
A SHAM, YOU SAY? BUT I'M A FOUR-LEAF CLOVER KINDA GUY.
NOT YOUR LUCKY DAY, CLOWN.

YA GOT IT ALL WRONG. MY PUDDIN' WOULDN'T GO ALL CLYDE WITHOUT HIS BONNIE.
I'M AFRAID MY DIZZY DAME IS RIGHT. I JUST CHECKED OUT FROM ARKHAM ON A CLEAN BILL OF HEALTH. I HAVEN'T EVEN UNPACKED YET!
SANE

I DIDN'T KNOW THERE WAS A BACK SEAT IN HERE.
I SEEM TO BE MISSING A SEATBELT.
THAT'S CUZ UGLY HERE IS WEARING TWO OF THEM.
SAFETY FIRST, I ALWAYS SAY!
ORACLE! HAVE ANY OTHER BANKS BEEN HIT?
POSSIBLY THE SAVINGS & LOAN OR THE CREDIT UNION?
YES...

"...BUT NOT ANY VAULTS YOU WERE THINKING OF."
Iceberg
CHECK IT OUT! PENGUINS **AND** SEALS?! *HMMMM...*
ARR ARR
AWWW!
NO MORE PETS, DAMIAN.
THIS IS AN OUTRAGE! WHAT FOOLS **DARE** STEAL FROM THE ALMIGHTY COBBLEPOT?
BE WARNED. THEY'VE JUST EARNED THEMSELVES AN ENEMY THIS DAY.
WHAT DO YOU BOTH HAVE TO SAY FOR YOURSELVES? YOU WORK FOR THE GOOD CITIZENS OF GOTHAM. HOP TO IT AND FIND WHO DID THIS AND BRING BACK MY STOLEN ITEMS.
YOU'RE RIGHT, OSWALDO. WE DO WORK FOR THE **GOOD** PEOPLE. YOU'RE THE EXCEPTION.
ARE YOU SURE YOU WANT US TO FIND ALL THE ITEMS TAKEN?
DOES THAT INCLUDE THE ILLEGAL BONDS, COUNTERFEITS, AND ARMS THAT MIGHT TURN UP?
GULP
ON SECOND THOUGHT...*UM*... NEVER MIND?
I HAD NO IDEA--
WE KNOW, RIGHT?! *BACK SEATS!!*

I PREFER A DOUBLE-WIDE OCCUPANCY.
THIS CONSTITUTES ANIMAL ABUSE!
THE TREATMENT HERE STINKS!
YOU GUYS ARE ALL NUTS. DOUGH NUTS... YUMMM!
I THINK THAT'S ALL OF THEM. THE POLICE JAIL IS RUNNING OUT OF ROOM.
THAT'S BECAUSE, IT REALLY WAS LEPRECHAUNS. WHY WON'T ANYONE LISTEN TO ME?
ALSO...I'M HUNGRY.
WITH ALL THE CRAZY CRIMINALS WE'VE FOUGHT IN GOTHAM, WOULD HOLIDAY-INSPIRED ONES BE OUT OF THE QUESTION?
I'M NOT WILLING TO ACCEPT THAT JUST YET.
WE'RE MISSING SOMETHING. JUST HAVE TO DIG DEEPER.
I'M PULLING UP A MAP OF ALL THE BANKS THAT HAVE BEEN HIT.

WELP, I'VE GOT NUTHIN'. WHO'S UP FOR FIXING ME A SANDWICH?
PEANUT BUTTER AND BANANA. MY FAVORITE.
MY WORD! DON'T YOU SEE IT?
IT'S VERY APPROPRIATELY THEMED FOR TODAY.
I'M NOT FOLLOWING.
IF YOU CONNECT THE DOTS, IT FORMS A RAINBOW.
AND YOU KNOW WHAT'S AT THE END OF THOSE, DON'T YOU, MASTER BRUCE?
BLEEP
HAH! I'LL TAKE MY VICTORY SAMMICH IN A TO-GO BAG.
KID WAS RIGHT AFTER ALL. IT WAS LEPRECHAUNS.
THESE BURGERS WILL NOT GO TO WASTE...
HMMM... LITTLE GREEN MEN...
HE'S NOT QUITE A LEPRECHAUN, BUT I NOW KNOW WHERE HE'S HIDING.

GOTHAM HARBOR...
POT 'O GOLD
GOOD THINGS COME TO THOSE WHO WAIT. BUT BETTER THINGS COME TO THOSE THAT TAKE WOULDN'T YOU AGREE, BATMAN?
NO. THIS HOLIDAY IS OVER. AND SO IS YOUR DAY OF THIEVING...
...RIDDLER!
YOU'RE WELCOME, BATMAN. THAT'S RIGHT. YOU SHOULD BE THANKING ME FOR HELPING YOU CLEAN UP GOTHAM. I'M A BETTER DARK KNIGHT THAN YOU.
I SUPPLIED YOU ALL WITH THE MEANS TO ROUND UP EVERY LAST CRIMINAL IN THE CITY. ALL FOR A SMALL FEE, PROVIDED BY THE BANKS, OF COURSE.

WE'VE SEIZED ALL YOUR ACCOUNTS AND TRACKED DOWN ALL THE MONEY YOU'VE TAKEN. IT'S NOW BEING RETURNED TO THE BANKS.
ONLY ONE LAST THING TO BE SETTLED. BUT WE'RE GOING TO LEAVE THAT TO THOSE YOU UNJUSTLY IMPRISONED.
YOU'RE NOT JUST GOING TO LEAVE ME, ARE YOU, BATMAN? BATMAN!
...THEY'RE ALWAYS AFTER ME POT O' GOLD.
STICK AROUND AND SEE WHAT HATCHES FOR EASTER, IN THE NEXT CHAPTER OF BATMAN: LI'L GOTHAM!

EASTER

THROWING?! CHEESE MOVE!
PONNG
METROPOLIS THROW DOWN
SUPERMAN
LEXLUTHOR

BLAM!
DON'T CALL IT A COMEBACK, BALDY!
FRZLAPP
METROPOLIS THROW DOWN
SUPERMAN
LEXLUTHOR

HOW ARE YOU EVEN SUPERMAN'S NUMBER-ONE VILLAIN?! A ROBOSUIT?!
WE HAVE LIKE...EIGHT OF THOSE IN THE BATCAVE!
KLANK
METROPOLIS THROW DOWN
SUPERMAN
LEXLUTHOR

OOH, SNAP...!
COME AT ME, THEN! YOU JUST MADE ME BRING THE BAT TO THE GAME!
CLUD
BATMAN
SUPERMAN
METROPOLIS THROW DOWN
DARKSEID
LEXLUTHOR

OH, DEAR. YOU'RE NOT A BAT. YOU'RE A BIRD.
JOKER?! KINDA EARLY FOR APRIL FOOL'S.
BUT YOU BETTER NOT BE LATE...FOR A VERY IMPORTANT DATE.
SYSTEM CRASH ERROR

AND THE JOKE'S ON YOU. NO CLOWNS HERE.
BUT THAT DOESN'T MAKE ME ANY LESS MAD.
MAD HATTER!
WHY IS A ROBIN LIKE A WRITING-DESK? GIVE UP?
THEY BOTH BLOW UP THE SAME WAY... TEE HEE!
THAT MADE NO SENSE. I DON'T GET IT.
YOU BETTER GET IT. THE BOMB, THAT IS, THAT I'VE HIDDEN IN GOTHAM ON THIS SPECIAL DAY. AND YOU'VE ONLY GOT AN HOUR TO FIND IT.
JUST FOLLOW THE WHITE RABBIT...
ROBIN! FINISH YOUR CHOCOLATES! LET'S GO!
WHERE TO?
WE'RE GOING DANCING.

A HOP, SKIP, AND BATMOBILE RIDE AWAY.
CLUB WONDER
UMM... AM I OLD ENOUGH TO BE HERE?
DON'T WORRY. I'LL BE YOUR CHAPERONE.
CHIKA-BOOM CHIKA-BOOM
THERE HE IS. UP THERE!
-BOOM CHIKA-BOOM CHIKA-BOOM CHIKA-BOO
THIS IS "DJ MADHAT" COMMANDING YOU TO DANCE TILL THEY DROP. STOMP ALL OVER THE BAT AND HIS BOY!
WHY ARE THEY DANCING LIKE THAT?
IT'S... VAGUELY FAMILIAR...
CHIKA-BOOM CHIKA-BOOM CHIKA-BOOM CHIKA-BOOM CHIKA-BO
I'VE HAD ENOUGH OF THIS RAVE AND THIS LUNATIC.
-BOOM CHIKA-BOOM CHIKA-BOO
KNIGHT--
--NIGHT!
KNOCK

"IN A WONDERLAND THEY LIE, DREAMING AS THE DAYS GO BY, DREAMING AS THE SUMMERS DIE..."
UNGH... MAD HATTER?
KEEP YOUR TEMPER.
YES...WE'RE ALL MAD HERE.
AH, YOU'VE COME TO YOUR SENSES. YOUR NON-SENSES. NOW YOU'LL FIT RIGHT IN. FITS AND GIGGLES.
EVERYTHING IS FUNNY... WHEN YOU CAN LAUGH AT IT. TEE HEE!
HAHAHAHA!
EAT ME
EAT ME
UMM... HOW AM I SUPPOSED TO DRINK THIS?
CAREFULLY. AND THAT'S THE TOOTH, THE WHOLE TOOTH, AND NOTHING BUT THE TOOTH.
CURIOUSER AND CURIOUSER.
CURIOSITY KILLED THE CAT, TETCH.
MEEW
POOF
CATERPILLAR... BUG OFF!
COUGH COUGH
PISH POSH! YOU DID THIS ALL WRONG, YOU DID. YOU DIDN'T LISTEN TO ME. THERE ARE NO WHITE RABBITS HERE.
YOU'VE FAILED. YOU'VE BOMBED.

WHITE RABBIT...YOU MEAN THE EASTER BUNNY?
OF COURSE! THE YEARLY EASTER EGG HUNT AT GOTHAM CENTRAL PARK.

THAT'S WHERE THEY HID THE BOMB.

TEATIME IS OVER.
HOPE YOU SAVED ROOM FOR SOME KNUCKLE CAKES, LOSERS!
RIIIP

SMOKING IS BAD FOR YOU!
KRAK
ROBIN, GO FIND THE BOMB!

I'LL TAKE CARE OF THE GANG, STARTING WITH TWEEDLE DON'T.
OOOOOW!
BONK

GOTHAM CENTRAL PARK.
FOUND YAH!
TIME TO CROSS ANOTHER OFF MY BUCKET LIST. NEXT UP... THE TOOTH FAIRY AND SANTA.
CRIK
THOOM
YOU'RE GOING DOWN, BOMB BUNNY!
WHERE'S THE EXPLOSIVES?
WHAT?! I DON'T KNOW. I WAS JUST HIRED TO BE HERE TO ENTERTAIN THE KIDS.
FORGET IT. I'LL FIND IT MYSELF!
FIND WHAT?!
NOPE, NOT THIS ONE.
NO TICKING HERE, EITHER.

HIPPITY-HOP TO HIM AND GET MAD...
MAD AS A MARCH HARE!
BRING IT, HONEY BUNNY.
KLIK
TIME TA CLOCK OUT, BATS!
HOLD STILL!
MY THOUGHTS EXACTLY.
HARE TODAY, GONE TOMORROW.
PIPP
MAYBE SO. BUT TIME MARCHES ON. YOU'LL NEVER STOP HIM.
YOU'RE RIGHT...
YOUR CLOCK HAS RUN OUT.

"...BUT I WON'T HAVE TO."
THIS IS USELESS. I'M RUNNING OUT OF EGGS.
UNLESS...
I'LL TAKE THAT BASKET.
AND THAT ONE.
GIMME THAT ONE, TOO.
WAAAH!
MOMMEEEE!!
ROBIN TOOK MY EGGS!
LITTLE BUNNY FOO FOO...
...HOPPING THROUGH THE FOREST...
...SCOOPING UP THE FIELD MICE...

"...AND BOPPIN' 'EM ON THE HEAD!"
BAM
BAM
BAM
HEY!
QUIT THAT, YOU ZOMBUNNIES!
BEING CONTROLLED...BY MAD HATTER...
...TOO MANY OF THEM...
TICK
TICK
TICK
WAIT...IS THAT...
...JUST GOTTA REACH IT...
TIIICK

"I'D GIVE ALL THE WEALTH THAT YEARS HAVE PILED, THE SLOW RESULT OF LIFE'S DECAY, TO BE ONCE MORE A LITTLE CHILD FOR ONE BRIGHT SUMMER DAY."
BLIP
HOW DID YOU FIND ME, SILLY BAT?
I FOUND YOU WITH YOUR SILLY HAT.
Parkside BISTRO
THE KIDS ARE NO LONGER UNDER YOUR CONTROL, TETCH.
AND THE BOMB?!

MENU
I'D BE CAREFUL EATING THAT IF I WERE YOU. THERE'S A NEW COOK IN THE KITCHEN...

...USING A SPECIAL BATCH OF EGGS.
GULP!
TICK
TICK
TICK
HAPPY EASTER!
JOIN US FOR THE NEXT ISSUE OF BATMAN: LI'L GOTHAM IN APRIL AS WE SHOWER GOTHAM WITH MORE SEASONAL SPIRIT!

APRIL SHOWERS

MONDAY
15
"MONDAY'S CRIMINAL IS FAIR OF FACE."
GRUNDY HATE MONDAY!
CRACK
WHEEEEE!
TUESDAY
16
"TUESDAY'S CRIMINAL IS FULL OF GRACE.
WEDNESDAY
17
"WEDNESDAY'S CRIMINAL IS FULL OF WOE."
FEAR... DESPAIR... BOO!
MEEP?
THURS
18
WHEW
"THURSDAY'S CRIMINAL HAS FAR TO GO.
FRIDAY
19
SATURDAY
20
"FRIDAY'S CRIMINAL IS LOVING AND GIVING.
"SATURDAY'S CRIMINAL WORKS HARD FOR A LIVING.
NOVDECJANFE
MTR
MADHBR
ARKD
MR KE
SUNDAY
FAREWELL Victor
BUT THE CRIMINAL THAT LEAVES TODAY, IS VERY COLD AND GONE AWAY.

MR. FRIES, YOU'VE MADE REMARKABLE PROGRESS AND ARE NO LONGER REQUIRED TO STAY.
VICTOR, I'M PLEASED TO TELL YOU...YOU'RE FREE TO GO.
HEYA, VIC! YOU'RE LEAVING US ALREADY? GOOD FOR YOU, BUD.
ALSO I WANTED TO THANK YA FOR YOUR CONCERNS OVER MY SICK GIRL.
IF YOU'LL FOLLOW ME, I'LL WALK YOU OUT.
PLEASE, GIVE THIS TO YOUR DAUGHTER. I HOPE SUZI FEELS BETTER SOON.
SNIFFF
FREEDOM!

GOTHAM CITY TRANSIT
ALL ABOARD! NEXT STOP, GOTHAM CITY.
YIP YIP
GULP!
YOU CAN HAVE MY SEAT.
HERE, TAKE MINE.
I'LL MAKE ROOM FOR YOU HERE, SIR.
YOU CAN SIT NEXT TO ME, YOUNG MAN. PICKLES HERE DOESN'T MIND, DO YOU, PICKLES?
YIP YIP
IS IT POSSIBLE? EVERYONE IS SO KIND. SO NICE.
HAS THE CITY REALLY CHANGED THIS MUCH SINCE I'VE BEEN AWAY?

HONK
HONNK
IT IS GOOD TO BE HOME. GOOD TO BE BACK WITH MY...
...NORA!
I HAVE MISSED YOU. NOW I CAN RESUME FINDING A CURE TO MAKE YOU BETTER.
I ALWAYS WANTED A PERFECT WORLD FOR YOU TO COME BACK TO.
THE PERFECT WORLD I SAW TODAY.
SINCE EVERYTHING'S CHANGED FOR THE BETTER, I MEAN TO KEEP IT THAT WAY.
TO PRESERVE THIS WORLD SO THAT YOU MIGHT EXPERIENCE IT FOR YOURSELF, MY DEAREST NORA.
AND I HAVE THE MEANS TO MAKE THAT HAPPEN.

THE NIGHT AIR IS COLD.
SHWOOOOOG
I SHALL MAKE IT COLDER.
WHOOSH
LOOK AT THE STARDUST, PAPA! EVERYTHING TWINKLES.
...C-CAN'T... M-MOVE...
VICTOR, STOP WHAT YOU'RE DOING AND LAND YOUR PLANE. NOW!
SOON, THE CITY SHALL BE PRISTINE. A WINTER WONDERLAND.
ALL OF GOTHAM. ALL FOR NORA.

YOU DO NOT UNDERSTAND, BATMAN. HOW OFTEN DO WE LIVE IN A PERFECT WORLD?
I HAVE CHOSEN TO PRESERVE THAT.
THEN YOU LEAVE ME NO CHOICE.
PANGG
PANGG
THESE SHOULD GET THROUGH THAT ICE SHIELD.
CHOOM
CHOOM
POOM
POOM
POOM
NOT A SNOWBALL'S CHANCE, BATMAN.
CAN'T GET COLD FEET NOW.
AUTOPILOT-ENGAGE
POOMF!!

YOU, OF ALL PEOPLE, SHOULD EMBRACE THE WORLD I AM HELPING TO PRESERVE. ONE OF DECENCY, KINDNESS, AND UNDERSTANDING.
CHKK CHKK
CHKK
FREEZING A WHOLE CITY ISN'T DOING A GOOD DEED. IT'S AN ATTACK.
AND WORTHY OF A TRIP BACK TO ARKHAM.
BOOM
B-BUT...I WAS AWARDED A CLEAN BILL OF HEALTH. AND MY FREEDOM.
I'M SORRY, VICTOR. YOU ARE JUDGED BY YOUR ACTIONS, NOT YOUR INTENT.
ORACLE. WHAT'S THE SITUATION ON THE GROUND?
PATCHING YOU THROUGH TO EVERYONE NOW.

NASTY CLOUD UP THERE. LOOKS LIKE RAIN.
HOW'S IT LOOKING ON YOUR END, TIM?
THE FREEWAYS ARE ALL GRIDLOCKED IN ICE. IT'S GONNA TAKE SOME TIME TO GET EVERY-ONE UNSTUCK.
HHH-HELP US! WE'RE FAR-FROZEN SOLID!
POOR FOOLS. NOTHING BUT WALKING POPSICLES HERE.
HMM... THIS REQUIRES FURTHER INVESTIGATION.
THE DARK CHOCOLATE DETECTIVE IS ON THE CASE!
STILL, THAT'S A WHOLE LOT OF RAIN AND WATER. A REAL APRIL SHOWER, WOULDN'T YOU AGREE, DAMIAN?
NUUUGH!
YEP...HE AGREES.
FREEZE WASN'T ABLE TO COMPLETE THE CLOUD CONVERSION PROCESS. ONCE THE SUN COMES OUT, IT WILL HELP THAW EVERYONE.

"ONE LITTLE SNOWMAN WAITED FOR THE BUS.
"HE CLIMBED UP THE STAIRS TO GO REJOIN US."
SSHH! TAKEN!
GRRR... TAKEN!
BOTH ARE TAKEN!

"ALONG CAME THE SUN AND SHONE ALL DAY.

"AND ONE LITTLE SNOWMAN MELTED AWAY."
TIME FOR THIS FLOWER TO BLOOM OUTTA HERE. LATER, FREEZY POPS!
ARKHAM
HELLO, LITTLE SNOWMAN. WINTER HAS RETURNED.

YES!
FREEDOM!
LOOKS LIKE SOMEONE WENT CRAZY WITH THE MIRACLE-GRO.
OH, THAT'S JUST GREAT. GUESS WHO'S GOING TO GET BLAMED FOR THIS.
APRIL SHOWERS BRING MAY FLOWERS? YEAH, RIIIGHT.
GCPD
BUT I'M NOT RESPONSIBLE.
LET'S GO, YOU GUILTY LILY. BACK INSIDE ARKHAM.
FREE? DUMB.

I FAILED YOU, NORA. HOW COULD MY INTENTIONS HAVE BEEN SO WRONG?
THE WORLD REALLY ISN'T A NICE PLACE. IT'S AS COLD OUT THERE AS IT IS IN HERE.

Thank you for the ice horsey. You are a nice Snowman. Love Suzie

HOLA! JOIN US NEXT CHAPTER FOR A FIESTA OF FUN IN BATMAN: LI'L GOTHAM!

CINCO DE MADNESS

ON YOUR MARKERS, FELLAS...
VROOOM
...READY, GET SET...
GOTHAM, THE BOWERY.
...MOVE IT!!
VROOOOMM
SCREEEECH
MAAAN...EVERYONE'S INTO DRIFTING THESE DAYS, BUT THIS IS WHERE IT'S AT, MAN. THE TRUE TEST OF THE MACHINE.
NO WAY. DRIFTING'S ALL ABOUT THE DRIVER! THAT'S WHERE THE TRUE TEST IS--SKILLZ!
THAT'S WHERE REACTION TIME COMES INTO PLAY THOUGH, SEE...
DO WE NEED TO GO OVER THE PLAN AGAIN?
HERE COMES COLIN!
VROOM
DAMIAN. DAMIAN!
YEAH, YEAH. FIND BANE. FOLLOW HIM BACK TO HIS WAREHOUSE. CALL NIGHTWING. BUST HIM FOR HIS ILLEGAL WARES. GOTCHA.

THAT. WAS. RADICAL.
HAHA! THE '80s CALLED-- THEY WANT RADICAL BACK, AND STOP BY THE '90s AND DROP THAT FLANNEL OFF ON THE WAY!
HEY, HOMBRE. THAT WASN'T A FAIR RUN. YOU SURE THIS THING AIN'T ON THE BOTTLE?
THAT'S IRONIC COMING FROM SOMEONE WHOSE CAR IS HOOKED UP ON VENOMIZED NITROUS. "VOS"...PFFT... REALLY?!
VOS
...
CHEATERS GET DEALT WITH HERE, MIJO.
LET'S
DEAL
WITH
IT
THEN!
HEH. IT APPEARS I'M NOT THE ONLY ONE ON VENOM.
BOYS, BOYS...LET'S TAKE THIS SOMEPLACE ELSE.
NO WAY! LET'S DO THIS NOW!
THE PLAN. REMEMBER THE PLAN?
BOSS? THIS BE REALLY CLOSE TO DAT GUY TWO-FACE'S JOINT, BOSS. LET'S TAKE IT BACK TO HOME COURT.
GOTHAM HARBOR. FALCONE SHIPPING COMPANY WAREHOUSE. ONE HOUR.
AWW YEAH!
EASY THERE, SIDEKICK.

TIME TO BRING IN NIGHTWING?
MAYBE EVEN... BATDAD?
COLIN'S GARAGE.
NO WAY, KATANA! WE GOT THIS!
COLIN CAN GIANT-UP ANYTIME. TIM HAS SOME SORT OF SIDEKICK EXPERIENCE...I GUESS. I'M SURE I CAN TEACH YOU TO USE THOSE FANCY SWORDS YOU LIKE TO CARRY AROUND. AND IF YOU ALL GET INTO MORE THAN YOU CAN HANDLE, YOU GOT ME.
HOW ARE YOU SO GOOD WITH CARS, COLIN?
--LEMME JUST OPEN THE THROTTLE UP A LITTLE... THERE!
THEY'RE EASIER TO UNDERSTAND THAN PEOPLE SOMETIMES, HAHA!
ESPECIALLY DAMIAN HERE. YOU HAVE A SERIOUS NAPOLEON COMPLEX, DON'T YOU?
IT IS MY FAVORITE ICE CREAM FLAVOR. WHAT'S SO HARD ABOUT THAT?
OH, GEEZ...
WHAT'S ALL THIS STUFF FOR, COLIN?
HE'S RIGHT, KAT. I TOLD NIGHTWING WE GOT THIS.
THAT'S STUFF FROM OUR CHURCH DONATIONS. THEY GO TO THE SECOND-HAND STORE AND THE MONEY GOES BACK TO THE SHELTER WHERE I GREW UP.
HMM...
WE'LL TAKE IT ALL! CHARGE US TRIPLE.
NOW THIS IS A COSTUME.
THIS IS AWESOME. COSTUMES TO HIDE OUR TRUE IDENTITIES FROM OUR REGULAR COSTUMES THAT WERE USED TO HIDE OUR SECRET IDENTITIES.
GOTTA HAVE BATS IN THE BAT-BUNCH.
CHECK OUT MY NEW HAT.
THAT LOOKS JUST LIKE YOUR OLD ONE.
WHATEVER. IT'S GO-TIME.

BATDAD'S CAVE.
IT'S GO-TIME, BRUCE. MAKE YOUR MOVE.
IT'S NOT JUST ABOUT LUCK, BUT PLANNING. YOU'VE GOT TO BE QUICK ON YOUR FEET AND DEAL WITH THE PIECES YOU'RE GIVEN. IT'S ALL JUST A GAME--
YES! NOW CAN WE GO OUTSIDE? KICK DOWN SOME CRIMINALS? AND RETURN TO NORMALCY? WHY ARE WE JUST SITTING AROUND?
WHA--? "NORMALCY?" IS THAT EVEN A WORD?!
RELAX, HELENA! ONE MORE GAME.

Backwards spelling this time?
NO!
VEEP

NIGHTWING, WHAT'S YOUR STATUS?
I'M HERE, BRUCE.
WORST CINCO DE MAYO EVER.

STILL WAITING TO HEAR FROM TIM. SEEMS CALM FROM UP HERE SO FAR.
SIGNAL THE MINUTE YOU HEAR ANYTHING.

NO WORRIES, BRUCE. I'VE GOT THIS.
YOU'VE GOT THIS, HUH?
MORE ROASTED HABANERO FOR THE SEÑORITA?
SÍ, SEÑOR!
YOU LOOK AMAZING IN THAT DRESS BY THE WAY. NOT A NERDY CRIMEFIGHTER AT ALL.
WHA--?
NERDY?! I CAN HIDE AN ENTIRE BATCAVE'S WORTH OF ARSENAL IN THIS DRESS. THIS IS THE PERFECT CRIMEFIGHTING COSTUME!
HAH! I'D LOVE TO SEE THAT!
AREN'T THOSE, LIKE...REALLY, REALLY HOT?
MEH.
BABS...YOU GOTTA PACE YOURSELF. THE NIGHT IS YOUNG.
NOPE. BRUCE CAN BUST US AANNY MINUTE, AND PEPPERS THIS DELICIOUS ARE IMPOSSIBLE TO COME BY IN GOTHAM.
MMLPH!
MUST BE NICE TO HAVE YOUR OWN SIDEKICK NOW, HUH? HOW DO YOU THINK HE'S DOING?
HE'S A BIG BOY. HE'S GOT IT UNDER CONTROL.
MORE ROASTED HABANERO FOR THE SEÑORITA?
SIGH
SÍ, SEÑOR. HAPPY CINCO DE MAYO, BABS.

CROOSH
NOT BAD, MIJO. YOU FIGHT LIKE MY YOUNGER SELF.
A FASTER, YOUNGER YOU.
SPEED IS GOOD, BUT EXPERIENCE WILL GET YOU FAR, MIJO.
HEY-- WHUTT?
PICTURE WHERE YOU'LL BE BEFORE YOU GET THERE. I'LL MAKE IT EASY FOR YOU. PICTURE ME WINNING AND YOU LOSING.
THIS IS SO BOOORING! THEY'RE THE SAME SIZE AND EVERY-THING! IT'S GOING NOWHERE!
TIME TO CALL IT A NIGHT...OR IN THIS CASE, A NIGHTWING. TELL HIM MISSION ACCOMPLISHED.
EXCUSE ME? DID YOU JUST CALL MY FRIEND HERE A CHIBI?
DUDE, I THINK THIS GUY JUST CALLED YOU A CHIBI.
¿??
THAT MEANS LITTLE... AS IN... SCRAWNY.
KRAK
YES!

THIS IS NACHO LUCKY DAY!
THOK
OINK
WHO WRITES YOUR DIALOGUE? THAT WAS ALMOST AS BAD AS YOUR FIGHTING STYLE.
I CAN'T BELIEVE I ACTUALLY AGREE WITH THE BRAT ON THAT ONE.
WUMPH
HORCHATA BREAK?
THOK
HORCHATA BREAK.
SNAP
SÍ, SEÑOR!
OH-HO! LOOK AT DE LITTLE ONE FIGHT. HIS HEAD IS SO BIG, AND HIS FEET ARE SO TINY. IT MAKES ME LAUGH!
OOOH-- NICE HAT, MIJO!
FANKS!
SILENCIO!

IT IS TIME, MY FRIENDS, TO MOVE THIS PARTY TO THE AFTER-PARTY.
AW, MAN. I WAS JUST GETTING WARMED UP!
ACKK
HEY! GET OFFA ME, YOU THUG! SO MEAN!
AMIGOS, DIS NEXT CHALLENGE IS ONLY FOR THE SKILLED AND NOT WEAK OF STOMACH. I AM UNDEFEATED IN THIS. PREPARE...
...TO MAKE YOUR OWN TACOS.
LETTUCE
HABANERO...
THE ILLEGAL WARES?!
ALL RIGHT... IT'S TIME TO TAKE THIS OPERATION DOWN.
OKAY. SO THE PLAN OF ATTACK IS--
I GOT THIS. THE "IRON" CHEF HAS ARRIVED.

A LITTLE SLICE, A LITTLE DICE.
SLICE
A LITTLE NOT SO NICE.
CHOOOP
SWIISH
STEP RIGHT UP, BOYS.
PLENTY TO GO AROUND.
DON'T FORGET THE SALSA!
ONE AT A TIME. NO TAG TEAMING!
CRUNCH
CHOMP
PLOOP
SEVERAL DOZEN TACOS LATER...
UUUGH... NO MAS... NO...MAS.
IT'S SIESTA TIME FOR THESE GUYS. THE COPS WILL TAKE IT FROM HERE. WHAT DID YOU PUT IN THOSE TACOS, ANYWAY?
SLURRP
NOTHIN'... JUST A LI'L CINCO DE MADNESS!
"SO WHERE'S DAMIAN?"
...NO MORE... T-T-T-TACOS...

HAVING A BLAST ON CINCO DE MAYO..HOW BOUT U?
GREAT TIME HERE. SO NOT A WORD TO BRUCE.
MORE HABANERO FOR THE SEÑORITA?
BABS...
SÍ!
~SIGH~
YOUR LITTLE BIRDIES ARE FINE, BRUCE.
NOW CAN WE GO PICK UP IVES?
IT'S...MAKE YOUR OWN TACO NIGHT IN ARKHAM TONI--ZZZ...
I HATE THE BOWERY. MAYBE CALL NIGHTWING NOW?
SLURRP
NO. I GOT THIS.
GOTHAM CITY TRANSIT
SOOOO... YOU GOT THIS, *HUH?*
AT LEAST WE'RE NOT IN COSTUME. YOU KNOW, THE OTHER COSTUMES.
BOK BOK
SLURRP
MOM
DON'T FORGET MOTHER'S DAY--THEN COME BACK FOR OUR NEXT CHAPTER OF BATMAN: LI'L GOTHAM. STUPID NINJAS...

MOTHER'S DAY MANIA

PAUL'S FLORAL SHOP
AAGGH!
HOW DARE YOU CUT AND SNIP. YOU CHOP AND MUTILATE. ALL FOR CASH.
THIS GREEN ON GREEN VIOLENCE WILL CEASE!
BUT I--I-- I'M AFRAID...I'M AFRAID WE'RE ALL OUT OF TULIPS. WUUH--WOULD YOU LUH-LIKE SOME ROSES? THE DARK NIGHT ROSES?
PAUL
FOOL! I'M NOT HERE TO BUY FLOWERS--I'M HERE TO SAVE THEM.
SO LET ME PROVIDE A FLORAL ARRANGEMENT FOR YOU.
NICE ONE, RED. YA MEAN ARMAGEDDON?
NO...
BLOOMS-DAY!
EEP!
LADIES, HE'S TAKEN ENOUGH OF YOUR ABUSE. NOW IT'S TIME FOR YOURS.
HOLD IT RIGHT THERE, YOU--
LOOKS LIKE SOMEONE BEAT US HERE. YA THINK IT WAS THE BATMAN?
WHAT I THINK, ROOKIE, IS IT'S TIME FOR YOU TO HURRY AND CUT 'EM DOWN. I'VE GOT ALLERGIES.
WACHOO!
PAUL'S FLORAL
IT'S NOT LIKE YOU TO JUST LEAVE THE SCENE OF A CRIME. ESPECIALLY ONE THAT YOU JUST STOPPED, "ABUSE."
OR DO YOU PREFER "COLIN"?

HEY, DAMIAN. WHAT'RE YOU DOING HERE?
I WAS IN THE NEIGHBORHOOD.
YOU AND EVERYONE ELSE--ALL GETTING FLOWERS FOR THEIR MOMS. IS THAT WHY YOU'RE HERE?
WHAT?! NO!
YOU NEVER TALK ABOUT HER. WHAT IS SHE LIKE?
WHAT'S THERE TO TALK ABOUT?
SHE AND DAD ALWAYS ARGUE. EVEN BRAINWASHED ME TO FIGHT HIM--THE ONLY TIME HE'S EVER BEAT ME. COURSE I LET HIM WIN THAT ONE.
"YEAH...MOM'S BAD NEWS."
"AT LEAST YOU KNOW YOUR MOTHER. I'VE NEVER MET MINE.
"SCARECROW KIDNAPPED ME FROM THE ORPHANAGE.
GAVE ME VENOM, WHICH MADE MY BODY SUPER STRONG. ONCE I COULD CONTROL IT, I TURNED THE TABLES, AND BECAME A HERO.
HEY! I KNOW WHAT'LL CHEER YOU UP. LET'S GO FIND YOUR MOM!
I DON'T KNOW...
THAT'S JUST FEAR TALKING. LET'S DO IT! YOU'LL FINALLY GET TO MEET HER, AND SHE CAN'T BE HALF AS BAD AS MINE. OKAY?
I GOT THE PERFECT WAY TO FIND HER, TOO. BUT IT REQUIRES TRUST... AND ONE A' THESE.
LOOK. DO YA WANNA SEE THE BATCAVE?
YEAH!
THEN YA GOTTA WEAR THIS TOTALLY SEE-THROUGH BLINDFOLD. WE JUST MAKE PEOPLE WEAR IT FOR FUN.
BATMAN USES KNOCKOUT GAS, BUT THEN WE GOTTA FILL THE CANS...CARRY THE BODY IN N' OUTTA THE CAR...IT'S A LOT OF WORK. JUST WEAR THE BLINDFOLD.
NOW WE BOTH GET TO WEAR MASKS!
FINE, WHATEVER. BUT YOU'RE MY SIDEKICK, OKAY?

ONE SECRET TRIP LATER...
ARE WE THERE YET? ARE WE THERE YET?
IF IT MAKES YOU SHUT UP, THEN YES, WE'RE HERE.
WHOOOOAH!
IT'S BIGGER THAN I EXPECTED. EVEN THE MONEY'S BIG HERE.
IS THAT A DINOSAUR? HOW OLD IS YOUR DAD?!
OR YOU'RE JUST SMALLER.
OLD OLD. NOT CAVEMAN OLD.
IS THAT ONE OF YOUR SUITS?
OH, THAT'S THE FAILURE CLOSET. THE OTHER ROBINS NOT GOOD ENOUGH TO KEEP THEIR JOBS. BUT I AM.
ARE THOSE...FISH SCALES?
WHY DOES HE HAVE AQUAMAN'S UNDERWEAR?!
HA! GOOD ONE. MY DAD COLLECTS EVERYTHING. COME ON...

GOOD AFTERNOON, MASTER DAMIAN.
MASTER COLIN.
WHAT'S THAT?
A FUGITIVE I FOUND IN THE PANTRY.
DESPITE WHAT THE YOUNG MASTER HAS TOLD YOU, I DO MORE THAN CLEAN THE CAVE.
I GUESS THAT *ALSO* MAKES YOU *BAT* MAN.
I TAKE IT YOUR OUTING TO THE FLOWER STORE WAS A SMASHING ADVENTURE?
...!
KNOW-IT-ALL.
AM I TO ASSUME A DAY OF VIDEO GAMING LIES AHEAD?
ACTUALLY I'M GOING TO USE THE COMPUTER TO HELP TRACK DOWN SOMEONE.
I SEE. BUT YOU SHOULDN'T DO THAT ON AN EMPTY STOMACH. SHALL I PREPARE A HEALTHY BALANCED MEAL?
JUST THE FOUR MAJOR FOOD GROUPS: CHIPS, JERKY, CHOCOLATE, AND LICORICE!
ALSO PIZZA SOUNDS GOOD! I'LL HAVE LINGUIÇA, CANADIAN BACON, AND ZUCCHINI. WHAT WOULD YOU LIKE, COLIN?
ANCHOVIES!
DUDE... THAT'S JUST GROSS.
SOME PEOPLE WEAR FISH, OTHER PEOPLE EAT THEM.
I'LL BE SURE TO RESTOCK THE INDIGESTION MEDICINE.

INPUT DATA.
DAMIAN, IS BATMAN OKAY WITH US BEING HERE?
YOU WORRY TOO MUCH.
"DAD IS OFF WITH THE JUSTICE LEAGUE, SAVING THE WORLD OR SOMETHING.
"THAT'S WHAT HE TELLS ME. OR WHAT HE LIKES ME TO THINK.
ACTUALLY... DAD IS ON MONITOR DUTY ON THE SATELLITE WHILE THE LEAGUE IS OFF FIGHTING. HE LIKES IT BETTER THAT WAY.
"I THINK HE JUST ENJOYS SITTING IN FRONT OF THE COMPUTER ALONE, NO MATTER WHERE HE IS."
DATA CONFIRMED.
WE GOT SOME LEADS. NOW LET'S GO CHASE 'EM DOWN.
HOLD UP! IF YER GONNA RUN WITH ME, THEN DITCH THAT TIRED OLD COAT AND HAT. IT'S EMBARRASSING.
THEN WHAT AM I SUPPOSED TO WEAR?
LOOK AROUND. I'M SURE YOU CAN FIND SOMETHING TO CREATE A NEW UNIFORM.
HURRY UP! I'LL MEET YA IN THE GARAGE.

THIS IS SOOOOO COOL!
WAHOOOOH!
BATMAN IS NEVER THIS CHATTY.
NOW I'M THE ONE BEING ABUSED.
THOMPKINS WOMEN'S SHELTER
I'VE NEVER SEEN HER BEFORE. I'M SORRY.
I'M AFRAID I DON'T KNOW HER. WISH I COULD BE MORE HELP.
OUR MEDICAL RECORDS ARE COMING UP EMPTY. HE WASN'T BORN HERE.
YOU'RE SUPPOSED TO BE MY SIDEKICK, REMEMBER?!
CYCLE OF ABUSE... CAWWWW CAW!
THAT'S IT, THEN. I GUESS WE BETTER TAKE YOU HOME.

SAINT ADEN'S ORPHANAGE.
HERE WE ARE. WE HAD FUN TODAY, DIDN'T WE?
...
SORRY ABOUT NOT FINDING YOUR MOM.
THAT'S OKAY. I ACTUALLY LEARNED ONE THING TODAY.
CROWS LIKE PIZZA?
THAT IT DOESN'T MATTER WHO YOUR MOM IS OR WHO YOUR PARENTS ARE--JUST AS LONG AS YOU'RE LOVED BY THE PEOPLE AROUND YOU.
THOSE THAT RAISE YOU, THOSE WHO ARE YOUR FRIENDS--*THOSE* ARE YOUR FAMILY. THE NUNS HERE HAVE BEEN GREAT PARENTS, AND YOU'VE BEEN THE BEST FRIEND.

SO, *UM*... HERE.
IT'S NOT FOR YOU, GOOFBALL.
DAMIAN?
HAHA, I KNOW. AND THANKS.

VSSHHN

JUSTICE LEAGUE WATCHTOWER.
SHAK
EERP!
TELEPORTATION ON A FULL STOMACH... NOT A GOOD COMBINATION.
WHERE IS DAD? THIS MUST BE IMPORTANT.
HELLO, SON.
MOM?! WHAT'RE YOU DOING HERE?
DID YOU SNEAK-ATTACK THE LEAGUE? OR JUST MY FATHER? HE'S ALWAYS USELESS WITHOUT ME!
IT'S OKAY, DAMIAN. SHE WAS INVITED HERE.
BY ME.

THROUGH ALL THE ARGUMENTS AND CONFLICTS WE'VE HAD OVER THE YEARS...
FOR BOTH OF US.
...IT'S EASY TO LOSE SIGHT OF WHAT WE'RE FIGHTING FOR. OF WHAT IS TRULY IMPORTANT.
WHAT'S OUT THERE? ALIENS? SPACE GOLD? THE ANSWERS TO THE UNIVERSE?
WHAT'S SO IMPORTANT?!
YOU ARE, DAMIAN.
I WAS HOPING IT WAS SPACE GOLD.
PSSST... IS SHE MIND-CONTROLLING YOU? DID SHE USE HER ASSASSIN WILES?
JUST WINK IF YOU'RE OKAY.
BATS DON'T WINK.
THAT'S MY DAD...AND MY MOM.

SAINT ADEN'S ORPHANAGE.
SISTER AGNES?
DO YOU REMEMBER HOW YOU CAME TO US? AS A BABY IN A BASKET LEFT ON OUR DOORSTEP?
I RECENTLY FOUND SOMETHING HIDDEN WITH YOUR BELONGINGS THAT I THOUGHT YOU SHOULD HAVE.
AND COLIN...THANK YOU AGAIN FOR THE LOVELY FLOWERS. GOOD NIGHT.
WHEREVER YOU ARE...
SAVES THE DAY!
FASTEST MAN ALIVE
RACE!!!
HEROES!
His name is Colin, please
Keep him safe and lov
I'm always
...HAPPY MOTHER'S DAY.
TMAN
MAKE A RESERVATION TO JOIN US ON THE NEXT PAGE AS WE CELEBRATE FATHER'S DAY!

FATHER'S DAY FUN

LOOK AT ALL THE PEOPLE! IT TOOK ME AN HOUR JUST TO FIND PARKING.
DAD!
LOOK AT THIS GUY. GUESS HE DIDN'T HAVE TROUBLE FINDING A SPOT. I'LL JUST WRITE HIM A TICKET...
NO, DAD!
I'M THINKING THIS NIGHT IS GOING TO BE MORE TROUBLE THAN IT'S WORTH.
DAAAAD!
I'M JUST SAYING. YOU REALLY DIDN'T HAVE TO DO THIS, BARBARA.
"DONUTS WITH DADS" UNTIL YOU WERE 10 WERE PLENTY O' FATHER'S DAYS WELL SPENT FOR ME.
YOU TAKE CARE OF EVERYONE IN THIS CITY. FOR ONE NIGHT OUT OF THE YEAR, LET YOUR DAUGHTER TAKE HER FATHER OUT TO DINNER.
...MORE TROUBLE THAN IT'S WORTH...
WHADDA YA FRAGGING MEAN, YA DON'T VALIDATE?!
WILL YOU RELAX? I'VE GOT THIS.
THE RESERVATION WILL BE UNDER "BABS." PARTY OF TWO.
I AM SORRY. WE HAVE OVERBOOK.
WHAT?! BUT I MADE THAT RESERVATION MONTHS AGO.
POPULAR RESTAURANT, POPULAR NIGHT. BEG YOUR FORGIVENESS.
I HAVE TABLE FOR YOU IN ONE...MAYBE TWO HOUR.
THAT'S OKAY, SWEETIE. LET'S TRY SOMEPLACE ELSE.
THERE IS NO PLACE ELSE. NOT TONIGHT.
AND IT'S NOT OKAY. AND WE'RE NOT LEAVING.
AH! IF YOU WISH, YOU MAY...
...SHARE TABLE WITH OTHER FAMILY. WE CAN SEAT YOU IMMEDIATELY?
OHHH, WE REALLY DON'T HAVE TO--
WE'LL TAKE IT.

YOU HAVE GOT TO BE KIDDING...
RA'S. TALIA.
COMMISSIONER. MISS GORDON.
MENU
YOU ARE FAMILIAR WITH EACH OTHER?
MENU

YES. WE ARE A CLANDESTINE ORGANIZATION OF SKILLED ASSASSINS WITH ROOTS DATING BACK OVER 1,000 YEARS, OPERATING SECRETLY HERE IN GOTHAM CITY TO UNDERMINE THE FILTH THAT IS THE RICH AND POWERFUL. WE WILL NOT REST UNTIL THE DECADENCE OF THIS CITY IS WIPED FROM THE FACE OF THE EARTH.
AND WE WILL DO EVERYTHING IN OUR POWER TO MAKE SURE THEY DO NOT DESTROY THIS CITY IN THE PROCESS, BY USING THE POWER OF LAW AND JUSTICE, AND ANYTHING THAT FALLS WITHIN ITS PARAMETERS.
AND I ALSO REALLY WANT TO TRY THE GARLIC NOODLE HERE.
MENU
OKAAAAY... ENJOY YOUR DINNER.

SOOO, RA'S...HOW'S BUSINESS?
VERY WELL, THANK YOU FOR ASKING.
THE IMPORT/ EXPORT BUSINESS IS... HOW SHALL I PUT THIS? BOOMING.
IS THAT SO? WORD ON THE STREET IS QUITE THE OPPOSITE.
"YOU CAN'T ALWAYS BELIEVE WHAT YOU HEAR."
"MY THOUGHTS EXACTLY."

RIIING
IS THAT MY SON? OR BRUCE? I MUST TALK TO THEM. I INSIST.
AND I *RESIST.* FORGET IT.
I HOPE I'M NOT DISTURBING YOU, MISS GORDON.
NOT AT ALL, ALFRED. BESIDES, THERE'S ALREADY *PLENTY* HERE TO BE *DISTURBED* ABOUT.
WHY? WHAT'S UP?
I'M CALLING TO INFORM YOU SINCE YOU'RE MY EMERGENCY CONTACT NUMBER. JUST IN CASE, SAY...THE MANSION WERE TO BURN DOWN.
WHAT ARE THE BOYS UP TO *THIS TIME?*
THE YOUNG MASTERS HAVE DECIDED TO COOK ME A SPECIAL DINNER.
YOU'VE BEEN LIKE A FATHER TO THEM. IT'S THE LEAST THEY CAN DO.
HOW DOES IT FEEL TO BE THE ONE WAITED ON?
A NEW EXPERIENCE. FOR ME AND FOR THEM. IF YOU'RE LOOKING FOR A WORD, YOU MAY USE "FRIGHTENED."
I IMAGINE BEING LOCKED UP IN ARKHAM IS MORE PLEASANT THAN BEING CONFINED TO THE KITCHEN.
IT CAN'T BE *THAT* BAD.
QUITE THE CONTRARY. THIS MUST BE WHAT A FULL DOSE OF SCARECROW'S FEAR TOXIN FEELS LIKE.

DON'T BURN YOUR WINGS, DICK. LET ME TAKE CARE OF THAT.
HOW'S IT GOING, RED ROBIN... YUMMM?
MORE LIKE YUCK!
CHOOM
THE ENEMIES AREN'T JUST IN GOTHAM, BUT IN THIS KITCHEN!
THAT BETTER NOT BE A DIG AT ME.
IT'S THAT EVIL OVEN. DID FIREFLY INSTALL IT?
OUCH!
HOTTT!
FSSSSH
THAT OVEN'S OUT OF COMMISSION. HOPE THERE'S SOMETHING IN THE FRIDGE.
EMPTY. REMIND ME TO STOP REQUESTING ALL FOOD BE FRESH TO ALFRED.
DAMIAN? CHECK THE PANTRY.
FLAP
FLAP
AAGH! THIS WHOLE HOUSE IS A CAVE.
WHICH IS KINDA COOL. BUT STILL...
THERE'S NOTHING HERE. WHO SHOPS FOR FOOD ANYWAY WHEN YOU CAN AFFORD A BUTLER TO COOK FOR YOU TONIGHT?
DAMIAN!
I MEAN... A BUTLER FOR YOUR BUTLER. SHEESH!
HALLOWEEEN! CAWW CAWWW

KRRRKK
WELL I GUESS IT'S TURKEY FOR DINNER.
GOBBLE?!
JASON! JERRY IS NOT ON THE MENU!
WILL SOMEONE CHECK THE BREAD?
THAT'S JASON'S JOB. BUT... UH... IT'S TOAST. OR TOASTED. OR BURNT.
CAN ANYONE SPARE A KNIFE?
MAN, MY SUIT REALLY NEEDS A BELT.
THOUGHT YOU COULD GO SOLO WITHOUT A BELT, DIDN'T YOU, GRAYSON? WELL, THAT APRON SUITS YOU BETTER... NIGHT-CHEF!
ARE THE BOYS READY FOR YOU?
IN A MANNER OF SPEAKING.
IF YOU'LL EXCUSE ME, MISS GORDON, I'M AFRAID I HAVE TO GO.
IS THERE SOMETHING WRONG, ALFRED?
NOTHING A GOOD FIRE EXTINGUISHER CAN'T HANDLE. ENJOY YOUR DINNER AND GOOD NIGHT.

WHERE IS OUR WAITER? THE SERVICE HERE IS TO DIE.
I BELIEVE YOU MEANT TO SAY, IT'S "TO DIE FOR."
NO. I WAS CORRECT THE FIRST TIME.
DR IP DRIP
HERE THEY COME NOW.
I'M GLAD WE STAYED. THE FOOD LOOKS DELICIOUS. DOESN'T IT, BARBARA?
BARBARA?
!

SPLOOSH
HOW DARE YOU INSULT US!
WE OFFERED YOU OUR COMPANY AND THIS IS HOW YOUR REPAY US?!
I'VE HAD JUST ABOUT ENOUGH--
YANK
IT'S NOT ME YOU SHOULD BE ANGRY AT, IT'S THEM.
YOUR NINJAS TRIED TO POISON US!
THEY'RE NOT MY NINJAS. MINE WEAR RED. OR REDDISH-BROWN. NOT BLACK. HOW HARD IS THAT TO REMEMBER?
I'VE FOUND ALL NINJAS TO BE BAD.
SOUNDS LIKE SOMEONE IS ANTI-NINJA.
I'M ALSO ANTI-POISON-NOODLE.
NEVER MIND! IF THIS RIVAL TO THE SOCIETY OF ASSASSINS WANTS A FIGHT, WE'LL GIVE IT TO THEM.
THAT GOES FOR ALL OF US.

AAAGH!
AWWW... I TOLD YOU TO FLY FASTER. WE TOTALLY MISSED AN AWESOME NINJA THROWDOWN!
HOW DID YOU KNOW TO COME HERE? I DIDN'T EVEN TURN ON THE BATSIGNAL.
...
DON'T WORRY. WE HANDLED EVERYTHING OUR-SELVES.
WHO'S "WE"?

I HAVE BILL FOR YOU.
AS MY GUEST, THE HONOR IS MINE TO PAY.
NOT WITH YOUR ILLEGAL FORTUNE. I'LL TREAT TONIGHT.
THIS IS A WAR WE CAN'T WIN. DAMIAN, GET OUR TAKE-OUT ORDER AND MEET ME IN THE JET.

I'LL ADMIT, YOU FOUGHT WELL TONIGHT.
SO DID YOU. WE ARE OUR FATHERS' DAUGHTERS AFTER ALL.

WAYNE MANOR KITCHEN. DISASTER AVERTED.
HALF THE YEAR IS SPENT CLEANING UP AFTER THE BOYS. WHY SHOULD THIS BE ANY DIFFERENT?
HOLIDAY NOTWITHSTANDING.
I DON'T KNOW WHY YOU GO THROUGH THE TROUBLE OF COOKING, ALFRED. WE SHOULD TOTALLY DO THIS EVERY NIGHT!
WHY CAN'T WE JUST EAT IN THE BAT CAVE?
SEE, YOU DON'T REALLY NEED LOTS OF MONEY AND A BIG FANCY MANSION. JUST A NICE MEAL WITH YOUR SONS.
TRUE. BUT WE NEED THE BIG FANCY MANSION TO HIDE THE BIG FANCY CAVE.
AND THOSE BIG FANCY CARS.
AND THE BIG FANCY DINOSAUR.
AND THE BIG FANCY PENNY.
AND THE BIG FANCY BALL PIT I JUST HAD INSTALLED...
...WHICH REMINDS ME, IF YOU SEE A GAS GRENADE IN THE PIT, LET ME KNOW.
WHAT WOULD I DO WITHOUT YOU BOYS...OTHER THAN HAVE A CLEAN HOUSE AND BE OUT OF A JOB?
BUT REALLY, GUYS, THE VENTILATION DOWN THERE IS HORRIBLE... IT COULD BE A PROBLEM IF IT GOES OFF...
HAPPY FATHER'S DAY!
THE OCEAN CALLS! JOIN US FOR THE NEXT INSTALLMENT OF BATMAN: LI'L GOTHAM AS WE CRUISE TO THE SHORES OF TOKYO FOR A MONSTER OF A GOOD TIME!

COVER GALLERY

BATMAN: LI'L GOTHAM #1

BATMAN: LI'L GOTHAM #2

BATMAN: LI'L GOTHAM #3

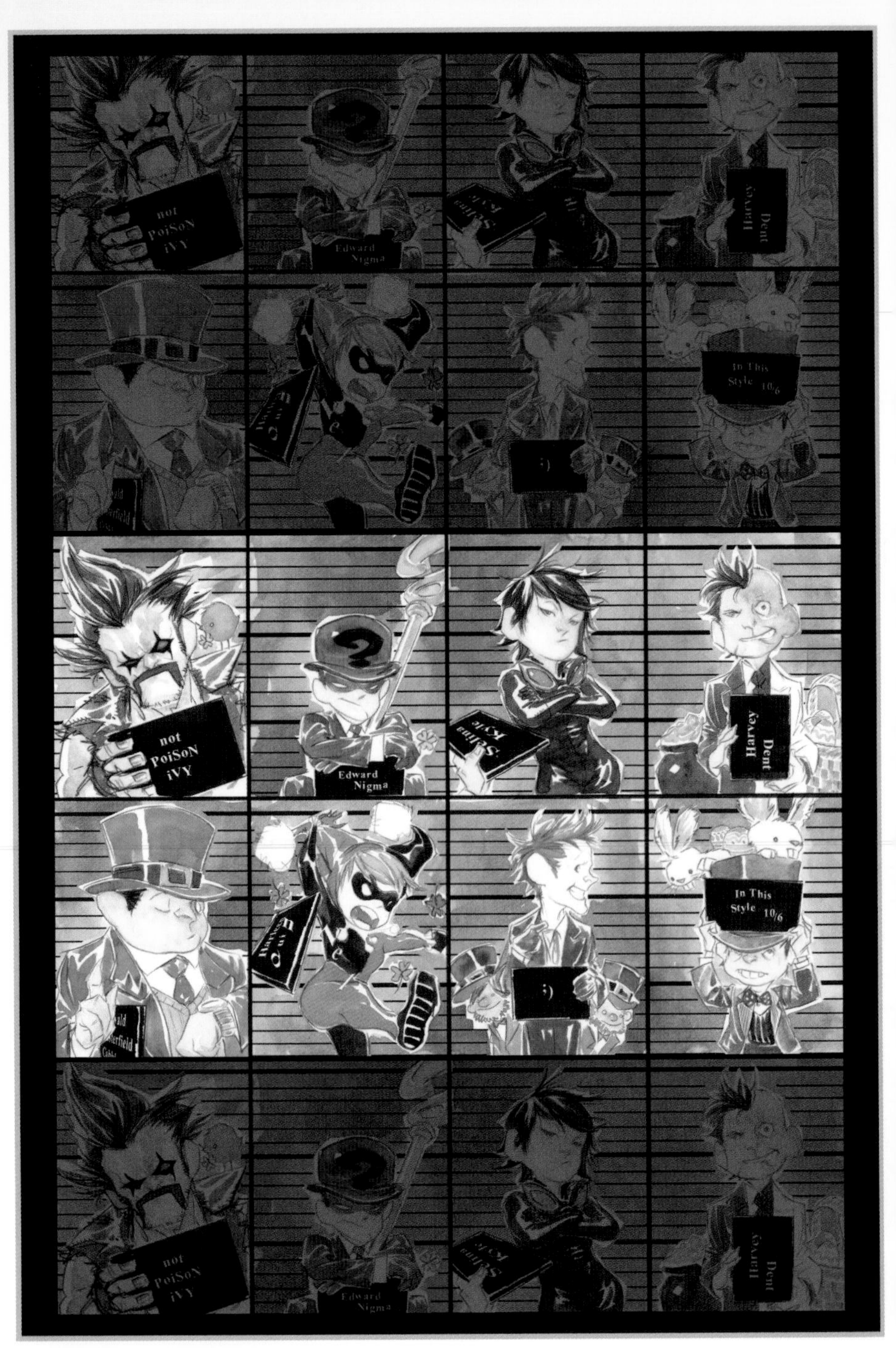

BATMAN: LI'L GOTHAM #4

BATMAN: LI'L GOTHAM #5

BATMAN: LI'L GOTHAM #6